It's How
You Play
the
Game

A Novel

Jimmy
Gleacher

Scribner

New York
London
Toronto
Sydney
Singapore

SCRIBNER
1230 Avenue of the Americas
New York, NY 10020

SCRIBNER and design are trademarks of Macmillan Library Reference USA, Inc.,
used under license by Simon & Schuster, the publisher of this work.

For information about special discounts for bulk purchases,
please contact Simon & Schuster Special Sales: 1-800-456-6798 or
business@simonandschuster.com

DESIGNED BY ERICH HOBBING

Set in Garamond No. 3

Manufactured in the United States of America

1   2   3   4   5   6   7   8   9   10

Library of Congress Cataloging-in-Publication Data
Gleacher, Jimmy, date.
It's how you play the game : a novel / Jimmy Gleacher.
p. cm.
1. Young men—Fiction. I. Title.

PS3607.L43 I88 2002
813'.6—dc21   2001049560

ISBN 0-7432-1626-1

For the occasionally capricious
and always captivating
Patty Stout,
and her boys,
Andrew and Cameron,
too

And may Harrison Kravis
rest in peace

It's How
You Play
the
Game

The game ends when . . .

My wife is very pleased with the house she just bought. We have sliding glass doors to a large wooden deck. We have a living room with a raised ceiling. We have two extra bedrooms, a tiled kitchen floor, hardwood floors, brand new appliances, and a staircase with beautiful railings. We have an incredible view of the mountains. And we have a security guard.

The real estate agent did not mention security. My wife is ecstatic. "He's free," she's saying. "Free security, isn't that great?"

I tell her it is. "Superb" is the word I use, smiling.

But there is nothing superb about that man, and my wife can't find out who he is.

chutes&ladders

The day has arrived. To my girlfriend it means everything, to me, nothing. And though a wedding is a wedding, I'm still having trouble grasping the significance, possibly because I don't even know the bride or groom. My girlfriend saved the invitation and the envelope. I think she wanted to make a xerox of the RSVP card but I sent it back before she had a chance. This upset her. I was trying to be responsible.

The presence of Miss Hope Witherspoon and Mr. Jack Wilson was requested as a "couple." Our first such request, upon which Hope said to me, "Jack, seeing our names together like this, I don't know, it just makes me feel so happy." Both the envelope and invitation had been marked with raised black cursive writing that was so fancy it was almost illegible.

Hope looked to me for a response, she was biting her lip; her eyebrows raised halfway up her forehead. I had never realized that both our last names started with W. "You should save these," I said. "Because . . . you never know."

And to that she smiled.

Now, as Hope and I sit next to each other in the church, waiting for the ancient (and judging by her glasses, nearly blind) woman playing the organ to strike up "Here Comes the Bride" all I can think about is a T-shirt I saw on our way here. It said, MY GRASS IS BLUE. Reading it made me smile and nod in anonymous accordance. But as I look at Hope, the gorgeous woman sitting next to me, tenderly holding my hand as she rubs her thumb along my knuckles in an almost suggestive fashion, it dawns on me that I have no idea what the hell that T-shirt means.

The organ kicks up its volume and everyone quickly stands, our heads turning simultaneously. Most of the crowd is young, like Hope and me, in their mid-to-late twenties. I recognize some of them from a party Hope threw when I moved into her apartment last week. Today's bride and groom were there but I never had a chance to meet them. The party had gotten way out of control in a very short period of time. Spiked Jell-O. Right before the cops came I was outside borrowing a tree trunk. I turned around while zipping up my pants to see a girl standing less than a foot away from me.

She said, "You're kinda cute. Mind if I borrow your lips?" Before I had time to refuse we were locked in an awkward embrace for a solid twenty-five seconds. The kiss was nothing special; tongue was involved, but no groping. I was more confused than concerned with my performance, so it's understandable that when our lips finally did part she wiped her mouth and in a disappointed tone said, "Sorry, just doing a little research."

At that very second the police cruiser arrived, no sirens flashing but the headlights were bright and I could see her perfectly. She was mildly drunk but the bags under her eyes suggested that she hadn't slept for days. And as I see her right now, in the back of this church full of guests while the ancient blind woman plays the organ from memory, I can honestly say that she looks much better. Being a bride suits her well. Her grass is the greenest it has ever been.

Hope squeezes my hand and leans toward the aisle for a better view. She sighs and rests her head against my shoulder. A common gesture but touching nonetheless until she whispers in my ear, "Mr. Jack Wilson . . . you never know." I nod, not to the notion of us getting married one day, rather to the sentiment that one never does know. The past year has been a case in point.

Hope's eyes are beginning to tear; she is beautiful, by the way. I put my arm around her shoulder, kiss her ear lightly and say, "No you don't, Miss Witherspoon; you certainly don't."

Last week, as I prepared to move in with Hope, I was storing some stuff in my mother's garage. Mom thinks I've made a mistake moving in with Hope. She shook her head as I unloaded a box of old dishes that didn't match, tattered sheets, and a disassembled futon.

"You're gonna want your own space," she said.

"Mom, I've pretty much been living with her for the past six months anyway, and besides, I can always come back here."

"Oh really?"

"Well, you always say you want to see me more."

"Are you gonna come alone?"

"You got a problem with Hope?" (Of course she does . . . Mom's got a problem with anyone who isn't my old girl-friend.)

"Sorry, I just think she's making you move too fast."

"She's not making me do anything."

"Where's the rest of your stuff?"

"My clothes are already at her place."

"That's all you're taking? Your clothes?"

"Yeah. My clothes, and this." I held up a small, white, hollow statue of Buddha in my hand.

"What the hell is that?"

"Buddha. Breach gave it to me."

Breach, the old girlfriend: cunning, pretty, shameless. Hope hates her though they've never met; and in this instance Hope is not being shallow, but remarkably instinctive. The simple truth is: had you asked me a few years ago, I would have thought I'd be moving in with Breach by now; and I'd be willing to bet that if you asked Breach, she'd say the same.

"Don't tell me you're changing religions too."

"Religion? She got it at a Japanese restaurant when she ordered a Mai Tai."

"Have you talked to her lately?" Her tone of voice is accusatory. I made a couple of major mistakes with Breach; one of them was allowing her and Mom to get too close.

"Last week. She moved back here you know."

"I know; she came over Friday night. Don't think for a second Hope is gonna let you guys chat on the phone anymore. Those days are over." Mom smiled the way pissed off people do, and she left me in the garage.

When Hope saw the Buddha enter her house she said, "What the hell is that?"

"You sound like my mother."

"Well, what is it?"

"It's a good luck charm. Where can I put it?"

"How about the garbage?" If Hope knew the Buddha was an old gift from Breach she probably would have said, "How about we run it over with the car . . . several times?"

• • •

The organ blasts and the bride and her father process down the aisle. As they approach Hope and me, I lock eyes with the bride. I shoot her a little wink, which quickly breaks all contact. Her dad notices and I smirk, probably because I'm reminded of my own father. Two seconds later it dawns on me that I'll have to avoid him for the rest of the night.

As I headed toward the bedroom, Buddha in hand, Hope called out from behind, "I did your laundry." Two piles of my clothes were folded neatly on the bed. One stack was all the stuff Hope didn't like. Hope's apartment is much nicer than my old one, but the design is upside down. The front door, living room, and kitchen are all upstairs, while the bedroom is on the ground floor. She followed me down the stairs saying, "I'm not sure if there's room for all of it."

"Let me guess," my hand slapped the reject pile, "everything but these?" My father had given me the shirt on top. In the ten years Dad's been gone it's the one gift he's sent. A custom job he designed himself, the T-shirt is red with black, furry iron-on decals that spell, SNAKE-EYED JACK!!! A present for my sixteenth birthday; he'd been gone almost four years. A postcard of Atlantic City came with the shirt—"Come visit," written in pencil, "you might not ever leave." The receipt for the shirt was in the package. It came from a local shop run by two hippies, right here in the center of town. It's likely Dad was in town and never told me. I think he comes around a lot without telling me.

"But I'm Snake-Eyed Jack," I said. "If I throw it out, how will people know?"

• • •

In an attempt to be different the bride is not dressed in a long, white, flowing gown, but instead a short, pale yellow satin skirt that does not go below her knees. She's got fantastic legs, and I'm considering the missed opportunity of our grope-less kiss. Of course I'm cleared of any wrongdoing concerning my commitment to Hope; had I known this woman was behind me I would have been able to react appropriately . . . I also would not have hummed so loud while relieving myself.

This first week living with Hope has been unsettling. Nothing in the apartment is mine—the furniture, the kitchenware, not even the broom. Hope's got pictures everywhere, friends from home, her mother, and most popular, her mom's dog, Slider. It's strange to be surrounded by photographs and knickknacks that have no personal meaning. It's an artificial familiarity.

Then there are those oddities that you don't discover until you live with someone, such as Hope's aversion to sugar cereal. The other day I was unpacking some groceries when Hope saw a box of Trix.

"You can't have those here," she said.

"I know. They're for kids."

"Seriously. I mean it."

"I'm twenty-six, Hope. I think I can monitor my own sugar intake."

She snatched the box off the counter, opened it, and started pouring the contents into the trash. "Listen," she said through clenched teeth. "Please, I don't want to explain."

I tried to stop her but she was shaking; her eyes began watering. She kept saying, "I'm sorry, I'm sorry," then walked out of the apartment with the empty box and threw it in the dumpster out back.

As the bride reaches the altar everyone quiets down. Her father lets go of his little girl's hand and turns around, nodding solemnly. The church is brand new; the structure looks like it belongs in an upper-middle-class subdivision. Not made from stone, but wood; no dark, stained-glass windows, rather large clear ones. The interior is bright and lively. The lines are simple and inviting, and though the feel is less religious, a commercial appeal has been achieved.

The bedroom ceiling in Hope's apartment has an opening to the living room upstairs. It's a convenient sort of portal; Hope and I pass things between the floors without using the stairs, but there's less privacy. This morning Hope thought I was asleep while she made a phone call. She was upstairs talking to her mom about our new living arrangement. "I love living with him," she had said. "It's encouraging he's so willing to make a commitment, but he's really loud in the bathroom."

I've never met Hope's mother but I don't think she likes me. Hope's voice becomes too cheery when they talk about me.

I got up and began to brush my teeth silently, keeping the water pressure low and drooling the foamy toothpaste instead of spitting. Hope opened the bathroom door and said, "What are you doing in here that's so quiet?" She was still wearing her nightgown, a flimsy, purple piece of fabric that's seventy percent see-through.

"I'm just trying to be a little less loud," I said.

She sat on the counter and pulled me between her legs. "Why? There isn't anyone who can hear you."

At one point she was screaming so much I stopped and asked if she was all right. After, I couldn't eat breakfast. The word Hope had used with her mother upset my stomach. "Encouraging"?

The bride stands next to the groom and everyone sits down. Hope is still holding my hand, her thumb still working at my knuckles as the groom shuffles his feet to face what will soon be "his better half." His chest heaves a bit as he takes a deep breath, probably in anticipation of the enormous promise he is about to make. A good-looking guy, tall, dark hair, athletic build; Hope says he's a law student. Apparently he almost got thrown out of the program because he failed his statistics class. His face is genuine and though he may not be a stats wizard, I'm sure he knows what "50 percent of all marriages" result in, and truly I am wishing him the best.

The best part of living with Hope is coming home after work. We play a lot of backgammon and I never win. Hope taught me the game, but must have held back on the strategic tips. Playing is fun; we always gamble though, so I'm constantly losing. Last week my hair was cut by Hope's stylist, Bruce. He had a great sense of humor, and after five minutes with him I no longer cared about losing the bet. Hope gave him a picture she tore from a magazine to use as a guide. He looked at the man on the page, then at me. With one hand on my shoulder and the other on his hip, he said to Hope, "Honey, with your ambition, you just might find the right man after all."

I've won once. The bet: Steak for dinner. Hope brought

the meat home, I grilled it; and then she said she felt ill. She put her hands on her stomach and made a sad face.

"That's probably the worst fake expression I've ever seen," I told her.

"Honey, sorry, but I'm queasy."

"You're making me queasy. I've seen better acting in porn movies."

"Oh yeah? Watch a lot of porn?"

"No. It's a saying."

"I've never heard that one before."

"Well I'm glad I could enlighten you."

"You don't have to be a dick about it," she said, and stormed downstairs. An hour passed. In the bedroom, the phone beeped as she dialed.

From the kitchen I shouted, "Who're you calling?"

"I'm ordering sushi," she yelled back. "Alright? Now would you please drop it?"

Today's bride made sure no bridesmaids would show her up. In order to be consistent with the bride's nontraditional yellow wedding dress, they're wearing yellow Capri pants and red satin vests. Perhaps these were meant to be "summery" colors, but the women look like McDonald's dancers. Their posture is proud and erect (like a crispy french fry), but I'm sure the phone lines were buzzing the day they received their uniform, which reminds me of another backgammon casualty:

I found myself in a large rectangular room with heavy carpeting and mirrors on every wall. As the only male in sight I was somewhat of a novelty, which must have been why an incredibly attractive, older woman approached me, told me her name was Merideth, and assured me that I'd survive. A hit song by a teenage girl, global in her popularity, though really more a marketing juggernaut than a singing talent, blared from several large speakers hanging from the ceiling. With my head down, surrounded by women in tights, lunging left to right, I vowed never to play backgammon again.

The aerobics instructor introduced herself as Amy. Her body was tanned and shaped in a way that asked people to stare, and I didn't protest. With an encouraging voice she gave instructions through a headset. I didn't know the jargon and was completely out of sync, stepping up while everyone stepped down, and vice versa.

The class was an hour and fifteen minutes long, and with an hour and five to go there was no way I'd last. But then a bead of sweat rolled from my newly designed sideburn. The cotton of my shirt began to stick to my back. A new song played that I recognized from a movie soundtrack. It was the kind of song almost everyone likes but few admit it. A simple, feel-good song; sung by three brothers from the sticks somewhere, who got their start singing at cattle shows. Now they're teenagers, millionaires and famous. I started to feel sorry for them but their song gave me so much energy. Merideth noticed and smiled. I returned the gesture and gave a half wave from a hand at my waist. With so many mirrors, Hope didn't miss it.

After the aerobics class Hope obviously felt defeated as we drove home. Her attempt to humiliate me turned into a jazzed up flirting fest. Then, to rub it in, because I was still bitter about Steak Night, I started humming the catchy song. "Jack, do you mind?"

"Sorry," I said. "That workout just really pumped me up."

She rolled her eyes, "You certainly tried your hardest to

impress that woman. I hate to break it to you, Jack. She was wearing a ring."

"Yeah, well, I was just keeping my end of the bet. When do we have to go back?"

"Sure you don't want to go alone?"

"Why? You just told me that woman is married."

Hope pulled the car to the side of the road and jammed it into park. "Apologize or get out."

I leaned my head back and laughed. "Hope, we live a block away." I laughed again, trying to diffuse the situation. "I can walk home in less time than it will take you to park."

"Fine then. Do it." So I carefully exited the car, shutting the door with the precision of a chauffeur. It may have been the exercise, or it may have been that I really was curious about Merideth, but instead of walking home I sat down on a bench. It was sunny, warm, and it felt good to relax. I shut my eyes, and I began to talk out loud to my friend Mark.

Mark is dead; a few friends and I were with him when it happened. We were so far out in the country we ended up sitting by him for an hour waiting for an ambulance. That hour meant many things, and I will never truly recover from the feeling of helplessness, watching my friend slowly die.

I said to Mark, sitting in the sun while the sweat from aerobics dried, that I had just had a fight with a girl I had recently moved in with. I said I was surprised I'd even agreed to live with her. We'd been dating nine months, but still, it's a big step and I'm not completely sure. I explained to Mark that normally this would bother me, but since his death I've taken a new philosophy of life. I paused to let him consider this, then explained my belief that as humans we are helpless to fate anyway, so I'm trying to worry less about all the decisions that arise on a given day.

At that point a high-pitched voice came from behind me saying, "Who're you talking to?" I turned my head to see a young boy straddling a silver BMX bike.

"A friend of mine, but he's not here right now."

"Where is he?"

"Dead." It was the kind of response only a kid could take in stride.

"Do you think he can really hear you?" The question was sincere.

"That I don't know."

The boy climbed back on his bike, shrugged his shoulders, and said, "Well . . . you never know," and he rode away, trying to pop a wheelie off a crack in the cement.

Today things were much more amicable in the car as Hope and I headed toward the wedding. I was thinking way too hard about the MY GRASS IS BLUE T-shirt, and Hope was giving me dirt on the bride's father. It seems the father of the bride is also the father of a five-year-old girl, who right now is presenting the groom with the wedding rings. An adorable blonde girl, button nose and all, she's almost too precious to be the product of an adulterous affair.

The father, a software designer turned executive turned multimillionaire, turned out to fall in love with his wife's much younger and prettier sister. The young sister had a child, which, following a blood test, was proved to be his. The first wife split with half the money, all the artwork, and a custom designed GMC Suburban, equipped with satellite tracking, an onboard computer, fax machine, and DVD player.

But the audience at the wedding has forgotten all that and a collective sigh fills the church, the blonde button-nosed lovechild the endearing catalyst. Leaning into Hope I whisper, "What did her mother do with the car?" A non sequitur, but because Hope was thinking about the same thing (as she sighed), she understood.

"You mean the Suburban? She donated it to a Top 40 radio station and they gave it away in some dumb contest. He *hated* Top 40."

"She probably could have sold it for fifty grand."

Hope whispered back a little louder, "Jack, there's a wedding going on. Let's talk finance later."

Though the bridesmaids are dressed as drive-thru attendants, the vows follow the norm. The mention of Top 40 reminds me of the song I'd heard in aerobics. Looking around the church, I wonder if Merideth could be here. Hope has put her hand on my thigh, sensing my growing restlessness with the ceremony. Outside the afternoon is tranquil. The sun is high, the wind is calm, and the grass, predictably so, is as green as the sky is blue.

boggle

(nine months earlier)

When I ask Paige what she's passionate about she says she doesn't know. Trying to help I say, "If you could be passionate about anything, what would you want it to be?"

"Anything?" She pushes her hair behind her ear. "How about everything?"

This is a blind date. She's very nice, pretty, and we do share some interests. But it's not going to work. We don't like each other. We get along fine, but on Monday our mutual friend will have the same phone conversation with both of us, disappointed to hear we didn't "click."

We're at a college bar called Second Chance. An Olympic dive with low ceilings and on the walls are painted cartoons of drunk students with bubbled dialogue about drinking getting in the way of their studies. The women are painted with oversized chests and the men are chiseled, despite their drinking.

My name is Jack. I'm twenty-six years old and sell advertising space for a newspaper. It's a decent job and I hate it. I spend my day pretending to be interested in things I'm not. However boring, the job teaches me to respect those

25

who are passionate about their work. A client of mine, Sammy the subman, is the best example. Every week he labors over what promotion to advertise. He studies the weather, forecasting how it will affect people's appetites. Snow means a dollar off the chicken parm, rain lowers the price of an Italian combo. His efforts are endearing, and I always leave his deli in a good mood.

Paige is telling me she wants to stand outside the *Today* show with a funny sign. Her body blocks the lower half of a cartoon behind her—a blonde, presumably dumb, saying, "Beer makes math fun!" She's sitting on a keg with a math book in one hand, and a cup of foamy beer in the other. Her breasts are enormous; Paige's head is in the center of her cleavage.

"The *Today* show? What would your sign say?"

"I don't know. Something witty and cute, not too racy."

"Good strategy," I say. "Keep it PC."

There's a fair amount of speculation concerning Sammy the subman's past. Two things are known about him for sure: He gets free advertising, and he tells the paper whom he wants to serve as his sales rep. No one knows why. Some say he secretly owns the paper but loves to cook and the deli is a hobby. Others say he's in the Federal Witness Relocation program but is still connected; these Mafia ties earn him half a page in the Friday paper, no questions, no problems.

Sammy works mostly in a back office, wearing V necks, talking on the phone. The guy I replaced got fired because he had bad breath. *"He was like a garbage truck driving through the deli. No way to run a business."* Before my first meeting with Sammy I bought a tin of the strongest mints available. Sammy noticed. I offered. He said, "Jack, what are these things? They're like chewing on a mint tree." I gave him the rest; every week I bring him a fresh tin, compliments.

Paige is discussing her *Today* show outfit and I notice a cartoon to the right of a guy sitting in a classroom, gazing at his female professor. The professor is lecturing on ancient Egypt, but the bubble from the boy's head has the teacher dressed in lingerie.

"I've got it," Paige says. "I'll dress up as America. The weatherman can use me as his map."

The thought of Paige wearing a cardboard cutout of America makes me sad. Not for her, but for me. This is my third date in two months. The previous ones were no more successful. One was with a twenty-seven-year-old divorced and bitter girl who hated the restaurant because the plates were too white. Nice smile, but the only time I saw it was when a waiter dropped something. Then there was the thirty year old who was very worried about still being single. She inexplicably fainted during dinner. I asked if she wanted to go home. She said, "Don't worry, this happens all the time."

And so now a blind date, my first one ever. People have tried to set me up before but I've always said I didn't need help. But I agreed to meet Paige, rationalizing that a friend's matchmaking is at least more respectable than a computer or personal ad. There's nothing inherently wrong with wanting to appear on the *Today* show, but putting on a costume, entering a crowd, and screaming for a weatherman to notice her?

"What about Hawaii and Alaska?"

"Oh. I don't know." Her face droops a bit. "Maybe I could wear antennas?"

"Do you know any young kids?"

"Kids?"

"Yeah, you know . . . little people."

A beautiful girl walks past our table wearing a short purple skirt and a T-shirt with a star in the middle of her chest. She's got blonde hair; the platforms on her shoes raise her at least four inches, probably taller than me. She looks like she's headed toward the deck, carrying an unlit cigarette in her left hand. She stares at me like she's about to call my name out.

"What about little people?"

"Well, if you know two shorties, maybe you could dress them up as Hawaii and Alaska." I smile but she doesn't laugh. "You could put Alaska on your shoulders, and have Hawaii kneel on the ground next to you."

Paige is silent so I take a moment.

"You said you needed something to make you stick out."

She says, "I'll be right back," and practically runs toward the bathroom.

I go straight to the deck in search of the purple skirt. The girl does not know me, but she probably thought she recognized me—I look like a lot of people. Brown hair, five-nine, thin enough, and a face not meant for the movies, but maybe a network miniseries or an after-school special in which I'd have a small role as the guy next door. I could water the lawn in the background, or smile at the lead as I back out of my driveway.

College kids pack the bar. Every boy's baseball hat is turned backwards or pulled down low, the girls' bras are pushed up or absent. Before I graduated I came here all the time. We'd come in a big group, standing and drinking next to other big groups.

The door that leads to the deck splits another cartoon perfectly in half. The half on the wall is a dean of students bent forward and yelling. On the other half a male and female student are caught together in a dorm room. There's no dialogue, just the caption: "Getting screwed getting screwed."

On the deck the star-chested purple skirt is smoking with a friend. The friend is plainer than the star but she's got excellent posture and seems comfortable with her role as consolation prize. I approach.

"Could I use your light?" I ask. She passes me her pack of matches. "Thanks," I say. "I'm Jack."

She sticks out her hand and says, "Hope." She motions to her friend, "This is Leslie."

"Thanks, Hope." I shake her hand. "I like your shoes. If I had four more inches I'd probably have a better job." Their eyes fall to my waist, then to each other. Leslie bites her finger. "You know what I mean," I say, "if I was taller." I strike a match hoping the flame might divert attention from me, but the burning tip pops off and hits my neck. "Ow! Jesus that hurt!" Now they're laughing. "I think I'll be going now. Thanks."

"Wait wait wait," Hope grabs my wrist and spins me back toward her. "Let me see your neck." She cracks up again, apologizing, but can't stop laughing. Leslie has to sit down.

I point to where it hurts. "See anything?"

"Here," she says, "Do this," and presses the cold, wet glass of her beer bottle against my neck.

"Good thinking."

"Where's your date?"

"That's my sister," I say.

"Sister, right."

"Nooo," I say. "She's my little sister, I swear."

"She looked really familiar."

"She looks like a lot of people." I hand Hope her beer. "She's actually about to take off. I'll come back in about fifteen minutes. Will you guys still be here?" Hope looks at Leslie. Leslie shrugs her shoulders.

When I get back to the table, Paige is sitting in my seat, so I take her old seat, knowing my head is between the two breasts painted on the wall.

"Who was that girl?" Paige asks. "I think I know her."

"What girl?"

"The one on the deck. You were talking to her."

"You came out to the deck? She asked me for a cigarette."

"She looked like she was rubbing a beer bottle against your neck."

"She's Pre-Med." I say this like it makes perfect sense.

"So?"

"I was injured. She was the most qualified to treat me."

"Injured?"

"The match tip hit my neck, see?"

Paige squints. "I don't see anything."

Paige and I both know we'll be reported on to the friend who arranged our date. It's like living on film. She's trying not to sound intrusive because she knows it's not her place.

"Really?" I rub my fingers against my neck, trying to look perplexed. "I better go check it out."

I have every intention of going back to the deck to find Hope. Unfortunately the deck and the restrooms are in opposite directions. Standing in line behind six other guys, I glance at Paige and see her talking to some girls at the next table. There's no time to waste, so I slip around to the deck. Outside Hope and Leslie haven't moved.

"Let me try this again," I say. "You got a light?"

They both look me over suspiciously. Nobody says anything for a minute; then Leslie walks away.

"Is there a problem?"

"Leslie was surprised to find out you were Paige's brother."

Hope shouldn't know Paige's name. It means she knows

Paige, and almost certainly that Paige is not my little sister. Hope puts on a look of nonchalance to say she's annoyed and couldn't care less about me.

"I don't get it," I say.

"I'm sure you're used to that," she smiles at her joke.

"Seriously, what?" I'm not giving in yet.

"It took a minute, but Leslie actually remembers Paige pretty well. They lived in the same dorm freshman year. Paige had identical twin brothers who died when they were little."

My suggestion to Paige about Hawaii and Alaska for her *Today* show costume thunders through my head.

"Oh no. Please tell me you're joking."

All is lost, so I cave into the honest approach, figuring it's my only chance.

"Look, I wanted to ask you out, but I figured if you knew I was on a date you'd automatically say no."

"You're right."

"So give me your number and I'll tell you tomorrow about how ridiculously horrible this date was. I promise plenty of laughs." Hope's body is slumped, she gives no indication of a response. "The date will be over." I look at my watch. "It's actually probably already over."

She tilts her head, squinting her eyes, trying not to show that she's giving my offer any serious thought. If there's ever a time to say something it's now.

"I promise, the story makes me look like a complete ass. You liked that earlier, didn't you?"

"Fine," she says, and writes her number down on the pack of matches that had burned my neck earlier.

Back inside Paige is talking to a guy with a ponytail. The table we were sitting at has been pulled against another table, and occupied by four guys all dressed in the same clothes as me: khaki pants and collared shirts. I kind of look like all of them, except the one who has a ponytail and seems to be in love with it. He straightens the bunched hair every few seconds. Everyone looks like they're enjoying themselves. I'd rather leave and not have to interrupt, but then Paige would give a really bad report. Introductions are made, although somewhat awkwardly. The ponytail is managed by a guy named Devon. Devon looks confused. Probably because he is trying to gauge whether or not Paige likes long hair.

I tell Paige I'm tired and going home, and suggest she stay anyway. She pretends to think, looking at Devon, clicking her tongue, then says another drink wouldn't kill her.

As I walk out the door, the lights are blinking, signaling Last Call. It's cold outside but the air is clean. A woman on the street is talking to her dog like it's human and understanding every word she says. Maybe she's right, but the look on the dog's face is pretty blank.

My mother has never remarried; Dad's been gone well over ten years. He was no good. A wooden Indian could have shown more love and concern with just the expression painted on his carved face. And though Dad could easily be replaced, Mom shows no interest in finding his substitute. I imagine her loitering amongst her contemporaries, faking smiles and interest, one eye forward, one roaming. The music would be soft rock but the lyrics would be the same; the never-ending string of heartaches and heartbreaks, true love and blue love, and then click, the night is over and she's left with half a glass of zinfandel and a poor night's sleep ahead.

Tonight I should be happy. I met a girl and if the number she gave me isn't fake, we will talk tomorrow. These games are ridiculous, absurd not only in practice but also in theory.

In ten minutes the lights will be on inside the bar, illuminating the cartoons, making them shine.

The woman tells her dog to shake my hand. He rises on his hind legs, extending his front paws. I grab both and the animal tilts his head, squinting a little, like he knows me.

sammy's rules

We live at the foot of the Rocky Mountains, our population is mostly white folks who kayak and favor Velcro sandals for footwear. The most urban feature in town is the home furnishings and clothing store, Urban Outfitters, newly opened on the cobblestone pedestrian mall. To make up for the lack of diversity, "social responsibility" is abundant. Bumper stickers seem to be the most popular method of community service. Freeing Tibet the most pressing issue in town, "Celebrate Diversity" the most ironic.

This pressure to act socially responsible does not bode well for Sammy. Rumblings about his being connected has divided sandwich lovers. Some boycott, and some pretend to, but can't resist. Others like the novelty of being able to say they get their lunch from a mobster. Bottom line is, Sammy's got the best food in town, not to mention the lowest prices by far.

Recently someone has been writing enigmatic protest graffiti in red marker on Sammy's windows. One morning I got to the deli before Sammy and found the message, STOP HOT LUNCH . . . DIRTY FOOD TASTES BAD. I took some napkins and a glass of water from the coffee shop next door, and Sammy arrived while I was wiping off the message. He said, "Jack, you don't have to do that. I'll get it later."

"Don't worry," I said. "I'm almost done."

"These messages, I can't understand? You know me, right? Would you ever say I was in the Mafia?"

I looked at him dead straight. Large, rectangle sunglasses with elaborate gold trim hid his eyes. "Not in a million years, Sammy."

He cupped the back of my head with his right hand. "You're a good boy, Jack."

Sammy might be dirty, but until I catch him unloading stolen lunchmeat from the back of a hijacked truck he gets the benefit of my doubt.

One time, DINE IN EVERYONE—JAIL AWAITS CHEF was written on the window. The first letter of each word was much bigger than the rest so from a distance it looked like, D.I.E.—J.A.C. Sammy said it had to be a coincidence.

Today Sammy's office is stacked to the ceiling with cases of canned diet soda due to an apparent shipping order mishap. We're discussing his ad. This week Sammy's deli is offering three free diet sodas with any foot-long sub. Sammy wants the ad to say, "Hey Fatso . . . Switch to Diet. 3 for Free, Only at Sammy's!" I tell him conventional wisdom warns against insulting your most dependable customers.

Sammy shakes his head. "The only rules you gotta follow are your own."

"But you don't want to offend anyone."

"Jack." Sammy smiles. "People don't eat here because I'm a good person, they come for the prices." Then almost as an afterthought, "*And* the quality of my product."

"Well it's your destiny," I say.

"Destiny?" Sammy lights the stub of a cigar and leans back

in his chair. "It's only an ad Jack, we're not talking anything major here."

I recently broke up with my girlfriend Breach because I fell in love with her, putting her in a position to hurt me. Now she's not. My mother was upset, Breach was not happy, and when they asked for an explanation I didn't have one. What could I have said? "I love her so now it's over"? Thinking back on it I realize how ridiculous the decision was, but Mark had just died and I was feeling a little reckless. I guess my leaving Breach was like evacuating a town before there was even a warning that a storm might hit, except that towns don't have feelings, nor can they move away and start dating other people.

"Besides, who else gives away three sodas?" Sammy's arms are stretched out to the side. "Nobody, Jack. Nobody. It's unheard of."

checkers

The night I met Hope for the first time at Second Chance, I happened to pass by Sammy's on my way home. Written along the bottom of his window was BE A SUPER HERO, DON'T SUPPORT CRIME. The next morning I got up early, went back to clean it off, and DON'T WAIT FOR SECOND CHANCES had been added. It may have been another coincidence, but the rest of that morning I felt like someone was following me.

Right now Hope's behind a tree. She's just standing there, swaying, with her hands behind her back. She's not waiting for me. I'm where I should be, seated at our table, on time. She consults her watch and pulls a cigarette from a black purse.

A waitress wearing five different pins on her shirt asks if I'll be having lunch alone. One pin features a mascot for a beer company, a bull with blinking red eyes. Another asks to ask her about catering and party reservations, which I do not. One is just a yellow smiley face. The fourth: her name, printed too small to read. And last: just the word, Choice, most likely not restaurant issue. I tell her I'm waiting, and ask if it's awkward walking around with all those things on her chest.

Hope is still behind the tree. I've been hiding behind a menu since the moment I saw her, sneaking peeks every minute or so, wondering how late she'll force herself to be.

Hope was surprised I'd called so quickly, we talked for an hour over the phone. At first she didn't sound too thrilled, but after I explained the date story, as promised, she warmed up nicely, laughing and saying "how awful" at the same time. She's twenty-six, and works for a local magazine, which I've seen but never read. The pages are mostly filled with recipes and articles about different ways to spend the weekend. Much of the magazine's bulk constitutes glossy full-page advertisements of pretty women dressed for the appropriate season. Hope's got a position in their production department, tracking and scheduling ad space.

Our conversation was mostly small talk, but we spoke for so long I'm worried about what's left for today, *if* she ever comes out from behind that tree. First dates are tricky, a lot of give and take. Some people aren't afraid to dive right into personal business. A few months ago I had dinner with a girl, and the first thing she asked was, "What's the worst thing that ever happened to you?" She must have read one of those books written by women for women. She was probably told the question would "help her take control of the conversation." I told her I'd answer the question when dinner was over. She didn't get it.

A few months before that, my friend Mark died right in front of me. He was driving on a dirt road and took a curve too fast. When the car rolled his aorta burst against the steering wheel. He drowned in his own blood. I was driving behind him but going much slower and saw the car only after it had stopped rolling. Mark was lying on his back about fifteen feet from the car. He must have climbed out the window, staggered, and collapsed. Thirty seconds of terror from the moment he felt the car begin to slip to when he made the decision he could no longer walk. I mention this only to say it could have been much worse, which is something people always do when someone dies.

We were way out, and it took an hour for an ambulance to arrive, then an hour to drive back to the hospital. I had to track his dad down at a dinner party two thousand miles away. At that point the doctors were still working on Mark. I imagine Mark's dad sat with his wife, both huddled over the phone in a small private room, praying and saying optimistic words. In the dining room the dinner party's chatter was doused because no one had any idea how to react. Some hostess cursed fate for causing such an event to happen on the night of her party, then realized what she'd just thought, taking it back a hundred times over.

After twenty minutes the doctors gave up, probably about twenty minutes later than necessary. The phone rang once and I said, "He's dead." The father's reaction was not audible, but those in the room were able to read his expression, causing one of them, a woman, to shriek with such an exquisitely pain-felt clarity that even after I jerked the phone from my ear, and even now, six months later, her anguish reverberates in my veins. His father then thanked me, which I remember thinking was an odd thing to do, but he'd have rather heard it from me than a small-town nurse he'd never meet.

Making that call was easier than it should have been. The words *He's dead* did not even feel forced. I was not alone; two other friends could have called but I volunteered. I looked at them and clearly I was the most able to do the job. I am not a cold person, but when my fingers began dialing the long distance number during the final peaceful hours of that summer's early evening, I remember wondering when this was going to get harder. It didn't.

Hope steps on her cigarette. She's coming in now and I'm wishing I knew something about her past. It's always good to know about a girl's background before a date. Everyone has baggage, and somehow I always manage to find it, especially when I don't want to.

"Sorry I'm late."

"No biggy. It's nice out here on the deck."

The name of the restaurant is Willy Ryan's. The patio is an enormous square, the tables all numbered and arranged in perfect straight lines. We're at table thirty.

Hope immediately looks off the edge of the deck to where she'd been smoking. I watch her eyes and wait for her to explain.

She takes a deep breath, looking away embarrassed. "I didn't want to get here first so I stalled a little. I don't know why I feel compelled to do things like that."

"It's okay. Actually, I just escaped from a mental hospital. I like to eat shoes."

The games have begun. I could tell from our phone conversation that Hope likes to keep things light. I'm the same way, so it was easy to spot my favorite tricks: Changing of topic, Deflection by humor, and Denial of knowledge. For example, if asked: What do you regret most in your life? Possible answers: a. Did you just feel a rain drop? b. Not pursuing my passion for synchronized swimming. c. I don't know.

But this is a date and there's something I like about her, so both our surfaces have to be scratched. Questions need to be asked, and answered. The waitress with the pins takes our order.

"Mental hospital, huh?" Hope picks up a menu. "My mother just got a dog. I think she likes the company."

"What kind?" I'd like to know what happened to her father.

"It's a golden retriever." She looks up from her menu. "It's only ten weeks old."

"Have you seen it yet?"

"No. My mom lives in New York. I haven't been home since May." She frowns a bit.

The frown could mean trouble back home, like a divorce, or she could just be disappointed about not having seen the puppy yet.

Table twenty is behind and to the right of Hope. Two women are having lunch, passing their plates back and forth. Obviously a mother and daughter, both have red hair and freckled skin, and the two are at odds. The girl is probably nineteen and judging from what I can overhear, she just broke up with her boyfriend. Her mother is trying to cheer her up but failing, and every time she looks away her daughter spits food into her napkin.

"How often do you get to see your mother?"

Hope's answer, "As often as I can," tells me nothing.

Behind me and to the left is table thirty-eight. Four men in business suits have finished their lunch but are continuing to drink. While I'd been waiting for Hope one of them signed a contract to work for the other three's firm. The recruit is in his mid-forties, at least ten years older than his new partners. They're talking loudly about capital punishment. A bald guy with a blonde goatee, the only one wearing sunglasses, keeps repeating the phrase *An eye for an eye*.

"How 'bout you," she says, "do you see your parents much?" She turns the tables having given up nothing but a story about a puppy. I have only been able to deduce that her mother is lonely, she needs company, and there's a reason. But the focus is on me now. Hope's got her hands crossed and waits intently for an answer. The waitress's pins jangle as she approaches with a plate in each hand.

"My mom lives forty-five minutes away, so I see her a bunch. My dad lives in New Jersey." The waitress puts our food down and wipes her hands on her apron. "Fry?" I hold my plate up and Hope picks one.

She looks over the fry and says, "It must be nice being able to see her so easily."

Behind Hope's left side, at table twenty-two, a teenage boy and girl suffer the effects of puberty and young love. The girl more detached, the boy clearly infatuated. His eyes wide, neck taut with attention, centered on his first true love.

Hope notices me staring. "Those two are adorable. That boy is so in love, look at him."

"He's bummin'. It's like watching a ship sail out of the harbor with no one on board who knows there's a hurricane approaching."

"Why do you say that?"

"Look at him. She's probably his first girlfriend, a neighbor he grew up with, shared bathtubs and everything. I bet they were best friends, then puberty hit, and wham, he wants to make out."

Hope takes another fry and dips it in the ketchup on top of my burger. "She looks interested. Maybe she wants to make out too."

"Maybe, but when middle school is over and she's got upperclassmen swarming about, she'll look at him and see the kid who used to run through her sprinkler in tighty-whities, not a prom date."

"That could be the most unromantic thing I've ever heard."

"He's gonna hate women for like ten years, maybe the rest of his life."

The girl cautiously sips iced tea from a straw, her hair neatly pulled back in a barrette. The boy finishes his milk shake almost immediately; it's easier for him to drink than speak. They're taking turns pulling nachos from a plate. Every once in a while they break to hold hands.

Hope reaches for another fry. I slide the plate in her direction. "I can't believe you're saying that," she says. "And on a date? What happened to you?"

"It's not bad living near my mom," I say.

Hope looks directly into my eyes, pausing to let me know that she knows I just changed the subject. Then she smiles warmly. "What about your dad? Do you see him much?"

I want to tell her everything. That smile, a knowing smile, like she sees part of herself in me and is amused by catching me performing her act. I've never met a girl like *me*. Usually my past either scares them or makes me their cause, something to cure. But Hope seems comfortable taking what she's given, making me want to give her more.

"I haven't seen him in ten years. He's a gambler. Last time I saw him he sold my plane ticket."

"Oh my God."

"I know. It was awful. My mom didn't want me to visit him in the first place but I was sixteen and had some vision of reconnecting with him. Kind of foolish."

"How old were you when he left?"

"Twelve."

"Was it hard being a boy and having no father around?"

"Better than a bad one, right?" The funny thing is, I've got both. Although Dad does not appear to be around, he is certainly successful at interfering with my life; and I've got little choice in the matter. I can lock him out of my house, change my phone number, not take his calls at work, but he will find me. He may not be the best role model, but he's a persistent son of a bitch. If there was ever a man who played the game with no regard for the rules, it's my father, and he will stop at nothing to win.

"So let me ask you a question. Who do you turn to now, today, if you need advice and you don't want to ask your mother?"

"You mean like a father figure? Easy. You know Sammy the subman?"

"The Mafia guy?"

"You don't *know* that. He's actually a really good guy; he gives me advice all the time. He's like a godfather." Hope starts to laugh, thinking I must be joking. I'm not, but now she thinks I'm funny.

Over the past year my father has sent me several letters. His writing is schizophrenic. Sometimes he's apologetic, other times he's angry. He doesn't always finish sentences. One letter read, *Jack, I've decided to . . . It's risky but if all concerned parties exercise . . . looking forward . . . don't worry, age brings forgiveness . . . Remember?*

Back at table twenty-two the teenagers have switched hands.

"I'm sorry about your dad."

"Don't be," I say, "you weren't even there. Kind of like him." I smile. "So what about your dad? Does he have any addictions or diseases you care to talk about?"

"My dad died when I was nine."

Behind me, and to the right, singing rises up from table

thirty-six. "Happy Birthday" is the song. A boy wears a paper crown, sitting like a king, ready to blow out the candles.

I look at Hope, stunned. Before I can speak she says, "Birthday parties were always fun."

Following her lead I say, "You know what else is fun? Bungee jumping." The men in the suits at table thirty-eight are finished drinking. I hear their chairs slide against the floor, and I can feel them standing up behind me. "I went to Great Adventure a few years ago and jumped off the top of a four-story crane."

I look at Hope to see how she's going to react. I want to apologize, but that would bring back the subject of her dad, which she just dropped.

"Wasn't it so much fun?"

"You've done it too?"

"Oh yeah," she says. "I jumped off a bridge in New Zealand that was five hundred and seventy-two feet above a river."

Our waitress puts our check on the table. Hope tries to pick it up, but I don't let her.

Outside I ask, "So can I walk you home?"

"Please," she says, "but I'll warn you, it's uphill."

"How far?"

"About a mile."

"Yeah?" Jokingly, "I don't know."

She tugs my hand, "Come on, it'll be good for you. Besides, these streets are pretty dangerous for a girl to be walking all alone." She tilts her head in the direction of an extremely short man sitting on a bench across from the restaurant. He's got a beard and mirrored sunglasses and his legs aren't long enough to reach the ground below. His T-shirt is white and says, I ♥ SUPERHEROES. He watches

Hope as she smiles at me, winking in jest. Then the guy takes his sunglasses off and snaps our picture with a Polaroid camera. Hope doesn't see this and I gently nudge the small of her back forward so that we can keep moving. At the corner I turn around to see if he's following us but he's no longer in sight; he must have taken off the second he took our picture.

"So let me ask you a question," Hope says. "Did you really mean what you said about those kids?"

"What do you think I meant?"

"That you think people are destined to get hurt."

"Wow. Did I really say that?"

"Think about it, true love, with the same person from childhood until death. Can you imagine?"

"Yeah, it would be great. Seriously, I wish them the best. If you want to go back I'll buy them another round of milk shakes." She laughs. "There's just a big difference between Ideal and Real. That's all."

Hope slows down but doesn't let go of my hand.

"Well . . . before I went to visit my dad I thought about what was going to happen. At first I was totally realistic, then I started thinking about the different ways he'd apologize and try to make up for the lost time. Pretty soon, in my mind, we'd already been to baseball games, talked about women over an initiatory beer, and so on. So when it didn't happen, it almost didn't matter."

"Almost," Hope says. "Sorry, I didn't mean to bring it up again."

We're at her house; she invites me in and I begin to wonder what's next. Her living room is well furnished with a glass table and matching brown chairs and sofa. "How about a drink?" It's only three in the afternoon, but it's Saturday so

I accept. She brings two and sits down next to me on the couch. The beer is refreshing after the long walk. A good way to wind down from a first date. Hope takes a sip, closes her eyes, and leans deep into the back of the cushions.

"Hope. I'm sorry I asked so bluntly about your dad."

She's still reclined behind me, her eyes closed. She finds her beer and takes another sip. "Of course, you didn't know," she says. "But thanks for saying something."

"You know, I had a friend die, and I know it's not like a father or a family member, but it sticks with you."

"Forever, I think." Hope leans forward and looks at me.

She puts her beer down, places a hand on either side of my face, and plants her lips, half open, on mine, leaving them there. She pushes back from me and opens her eyes. Consumed by some fit of first date self-disclosure, Hope says, "Halfway through my freshman year in college my mother sent me to an insane asylum. Not because I liked to eat shoes, though."

Remembering my lame joke at lunch, I apologize.

"I was actually quite sane but it was the ten-year anniversary of my father's death and I woke up with a doctor sitting in a chair beside my bed."

"What was your mother's reason?"

"She said I had self-mutilating tendencies."

"Why?"

"Watch." Hope picks a single strand of hair from the side of her head. She twirls the bottom around the tip of her finger a few times then plucks the thin, almost invisible, blonde string completely from her scalp. "That."

"That? For how long?"

"She had me locked up for four months."

"Is that legal?"

"No, but she made it happen."

"Well how are things with her now?"

"Fine. That was six years ago. But I'll never win with my mom. I had a 4.0 that term, still wasn't good enough."

She sips her beer, eyes on me. "So, you want to leave now?"

"No. I'm having fun."

"Fun? I'd hate to think what you consider un-fun."

"You know what I mean. It's nice getting to know you. Sitting here."

She leans in and kisses me again, only this time a little longer, her mouth a little more open. I get my hands around her waist and when she pulls away I give her only a second to breathe before pulling her back. I feel like a kid who just finished his homework and has the whole weekend left to play.

Now she's fully kissing me, and I'm kissing back. She pulls away to speak. "Jack," she says. "If you don't talk to me after this date is over, I'm going to make sure we both end up in an asylum."

chess

My mother is in a drinking club. Every Friday night six divorced women get together for wine. Most popular subject of conversation: new boyfriends. First question: How's the sex? Another discrepancy between the ages: older women put out. No time for silly games, they want to know if he's a dud in the sack, even if he is a doctor, although that might get him a second effort if he fails the first time.

Hope hasn't let me try yet. Five weeks is a long wait. We've come close a few times, always arriving at the same two words, spoken in the heated last possible moment, "Not yet."

A visit to Mom's might help. We're going Friday night. Hope will get a chance to meet my mother and encounter the drinking club. Some of the women have known me for years and will doubtless tell endearing stories about my childhood. I'll surround her with all that is pure about me and see if that works.

One story they won't tell is the one about the day I quit the track team: I was leading a ten-kilometer race, but my rival was right behind me. All nine and a half kilometers he appeared in peripheral glimpses; I heard his cheers more than my own. But I'd saved enough energy for a final kick so when he made his move I turned on the speed, leaving him behind. Thirty seconds into the sprint, with the finish line in sight, a foot from the crowd sent me tumbling into a wall of legs, dogs, and baby carriages. I lost, limping to second place, while Tommy Quartz passed me easily. Tommy's mother screamed for her son to hurry up.

But that day is marked by a much darker event, the day my father left us for good, the day I learned that just because you love someone doesn't mean you can rely on them too.

Mom threw him out for the last time. He'd sold an antique of hers for gambling money. Mom told me Dad hadn't even been at my race, but at a horse's instead, watching it from a platformed television in an offtrack betting station somewhere downtown. I remember feeling intensely jealous of the horse.

I was sixteen, smart enough to know better; but the bitterness from the betrayal was hard to outdistance. Dad had skipped my races before, but this one had mattered more. Someone tripped me so that another runner could win. Dad should have been there, at least to argue, if nothing else. But if he had to leave then, why was he so intent on coming back into my life now?

Mother won't like Hope. She still loves my old girlfriend, Breach, for which I can't really blame her. When Dad chose the horse over me, I got over the initial disappointment. After all, he was a bum. But there was something special about Breach. The stronger our feelings got, the more I feared losing her. Sitting next to her made me grin, knowing she'd soon say something funny, horrible, or incredibly vulnerable. Never insecure, she'd say how she felt about anything. She even made a lot of noise in bed.

Hope doesn't know the whole truth about Breach. She does know Breach exists though. Last Saturday we were watching *The King Is Dead*—a tediously boring movie—at my place. I'd seen the king die before, and knew it was dull. The subject was eighteenth-century England, and more work went into designing the actors' costumes than writing the actual script.

About twenty minutes into the film I said, "Sorry Hope, I don't remember this being so bad." Then we started making out. In ten minutes I was near the point of entry when the phone rang. I let it go, but my answering machine took it: "Hi Jack, it's Breach. Are you home? . . . No? O.K., well I'm just calling to say hi. I hope we can get together if you visit home. Miss you Shugey, hope you're all right. Bye."

Hope pushed me off of her. "Who was *that?*"

"I couldn't hear."

"I could hear fine, *Shugey.* Who the hell is Breach?"

"Breach?"

"Shugey? I mean really, Jack. You never told me you knew Dolly Parton."

"She's a friend. I swear. Com'ere," I tried to kiss her.

"I'm not kissing you. Tell me who Breach is."

"I just did."

"She's more than a friend. She calls you Shugey, and misses you."

"She calls everyone Shugey; it's actually kind of annoying. And sorry, but saying 'I miss you' is not an exclusive term for lovers."

"Lovers? Is that what she is?"

"No. She's an old girlfriend." I tried a little laugh to ease the tension. "We broke up a long time ago."

"Do you still love her?"

"Still? Who says I ever did?"

"Well, she's still calling. I know we haven't been dating long, but if you're gonna see other people . . ."

"I'm not seeing her."

"I think I have the right to know."

On the television a lonely priest was doing something that required no dialogue, just sullen bagpipe music.

Hope looked at the movie and said, "Why the hell are we even watching this?"

Every group of friends has a bad drunk. The person whose voice grows a little louder than the rest, laughs a little harder, and every once in a while says something foolish. This would describe Alice, founder of the D.C., the Friday night drinking club. In all fairness, none of them get too drunk, not even Alice, but she never fails to have a good time. When I visit I do most of the work, pouring wine, refilling wine, and putting cheese on crackers. The eavesdropping is worth the little effort it involves. The women know I listen; they want me to listen, demure about their escapades, but none the less proud. Banter is whispered only when Mom is the subject. Then they raise their voices to ask for more wine. I usually look at Mom and say, "You guys have been quiet a while . . . must have been a hot one." They all laugh and if it's near the end of the night Alice might slap her knee and shout something inappropriate.

Because Breach and Mom clicked so well, she's hung out with the D.C. occasionally. The group gets even more hushed when they talk about me.

Hope is in the living room now and the knife I'm slicing through the block of cheddar is making more noise than the women's huddled conspiracy. Normally this chore is done leisurely, giving them time for secrets, but tonight I finish quickly and interrupt the quietness.

Alice says, "Really Jack, chasing Hope while you're on a date? What a dirty dog."

"Hey, it's tough out there. You know that. What about the time you ditched the guy you took to your office party? Didn't he get locked out on the roof looking for you?"

That does it; the D.C. goes into full nostalgic swing. Not until Mom tells the story about catching me kissing my god-sister does a potential disaster seem inevitable. To slow the crew down, I pour the wine sparingly, especially into Alice's glass.

On the way to the bathroom, I hear Alice ask, "So Hope, how's the sex?"

After the roar Mom says, "I don't need to know, thank you. Breach gave us too much information already."

"Breach?"

Mom tries to cover, "Oh, she's just an old friend of Jack's. She comes over sometimes."

"Without him?"

Now Alice gets involved. "Well she's not gonna come with him, they broke up months ago."

"But she still comes?"

No comment.

Hope finds me in the hallway, just around the corner of the living room. "Jack. You're not telling me everything."

"I didn't know she still comes." A lie.

"How serious was this?"

"You know, I don't ask you about all your old boyfriends." A deflection.

"Go ahead."

"Look. We've only been dating five weeks; we haven't even slept together yet. These conversations will come." A big mistake.

Hope raises her voice. "What do you mean, 'We haven't even slept together yet'?" Alice, with her question answered, probably looks to the other women, befuddled, as if to say, "What's she waiting for?"

"Nothing," I say. "I don't mean anything. It's just a thing people do when they get serious. We haven't done it . . . so, I don't know how serious we're supposed to be."

She looks at me, then at the floor. "We'll talk about it later." Excusing herself, she hands me a half bitten slice of cheddar cheese. "I have to use the bathroom."

Sounds emerge from the living room again; a half bottle of wine waits on the kitchen counter. Breach and I never officially broke up; instead we just decided to "take a break." Last Halloween we were in a costume shop called The Ritz. Breach was trying to convince me to dress up as Princess Leia.

"I'm not a girl," I said.

"That's why it's funny, dumb-ass."

"Yeah?"

"You heard me."

She was dressed in green lederhosen, wearing a Michael Jackson mask.

"You might want to look in the mirror before you call anyone a dumb-ass."

"I think I love you," she said.

People our age often use the word *love* recklessly. Breach was not one of those people. That night I told her we were moving too fast when, in fact, I knew quite well I loved her just as much as she loved me.

She said this: "That's a cop-out, Jack. But fine. When you grow up, call me."

Ending the relationship with Breach was a good lesson in how safety can only be bought with loneliness. I laid awake in bed that night watching my father walk out the front door and living that hour with Mark again and again.

Saturday Sunday Monday: no action. Tuesday morning I meet with Sammy. WHO DIED FOR YOUR LUNCH TODAY? AND WHO WILL DIE TOMORROW? is written on the deli window. Sammy's outside with a towel. "Crazy vegetarians," he says. "What a waste, such misguided energy."

"She won't sleep with me, Sammy."

"Who? Your girlfriend?"

"Who else, Romeo? *I'm going crazy over here.*"

Sammy always laughs when I imitate his New York accent. "Yeah?" Still chuckling, "Why don't you take her away then?"

"You think?"

"Hey, *Romeo,* you want to get romantic, you gotta act romantic."

Hope's under the impression our trip is a tribute to our youthful positions in life. She keeps saying, "This is what's so great about being young, we can just pick up and leave for the weekend, and it doesn't matter."

It matters. I'm leaving work early. I've called numerous hotels, combed maps for the scenic roads, and fingered through travel brochures in a quest to find the perfect day-time activities that will lead, naturally, into the perfect night-time activities.

Hope hasn't brought up sex since we left Mom's house on

Friday. I've been sleeping at her apartment almost every night, and though she's not angry with me, there seems to be an unspoken tension lurking in the shadows of our conversations. Sunday she called my name in the middle of the night. I didn't answer. She called a second time, then told herself to never mind, and rolled onto her stomach. I find myself growing fonder of her. Involuntarily, my hand grabs hers. Walking, I bump into her sideways, just for the contact.

A scary thing happened the other day, which made me realize just how attached I've become. Hope was walking home from work alone, the sun had just slipped beneath the peaks of the mountains. The sky had gone flat, but not yet dark. Hope says a male (she couldn't tell his age) no taller than four feet walked up to her, pointed and said, "Your world is coming to an end." Then he ran away.

I asked, "Are you sure he didn't say 'The world,' instead of 'Your world'? Crazy people are always preaching about the end of the world."

"Maybe," she said. "But I thought I heard him pretty good."

"Did you recognize him? What did he look like?"

"He was short. His T-shirt said MY GRASS IS BLUE, which I don't even get."

We slept at my apartment that night. Hope asked if there was something I wasn't telling her, and was Breach behind this? Just beginning to comprehend her Breach paranoia, I said, "Breach isn't like that. Besides, she and I are way over." Then I didn't say, "On the other hand, I think my dad is possibly mental; maybe he's behind it, or the guy who writes on Sammy's windows. Maybe they're working together." Okay, so Hope isn't the only one who's paranoid.

We were curled up on my futon. I told Hope she probably misheard the guy and she kind of laughed at herself and said she felt safe lying there with me.

Hope doesn't listen to music in cars. Nor will she listen to talk radio. She's got a thing about car stereos, which she hasn't yet explained. It's undoing my agenda. Sammy gave me a tape for the drive, promising, "It'll make her looser than linguini."

Hope reads a newspaper instead. The route we're taking is adding at least an hour to our trip. The map marked the road's path in light blue, indicating a "Scenic Byway." She folds down the top corner of the paper and looks. "Pretty." Her eyes scan the side of the road for a moment, before she flips the paper back in front of her.

The car we're driving in used to be my aunt's. I inherited it when she died. She was clinically insane. The police were never able to prove she actually pulled the trigger, but there were no suspects for her murder. She gave me the car because I pretended to be her chauffeur. She thought she was the queen of England, and bought the car for its royal qualities. It's a Lincoln Continental, black with a gray pinstripe and gray leather seats, designed to drive businessmen to the airport.

My dad thought he should get the car because he was the deceased's brother and tried to take the case to court. The judge found out about his gambling problem and closed the case before it even opened. During that time I never saw or heard from Dad but apparently he was not happy with the judge's decision. The judge placed a restraining order, which banned Dad from entering my state for an entire year. No one would tell me what he said or did; all Mom said was, "Don't worry Jack, it isn't important, your dad has obviously lost whatever small mind he had."

The scenic byway changes from a straight road through meadows into a series of switchbacks leading up a mountain. The map shows a reservoir at the top. Hope's reading from the paper out loud, "A judge in Florida overturned a court decision allowing new investigations into how an air conditioning company may be responsible for an elderly man's death. I wonder how he died."

Wildflowers dot the meadow in front of the reservoir yellow, blue, and purple. "How about Sports?" I say, hoping the topic will make her lose interest in the newspaper.

"Let's see, the World Series Wild Card race is tied. Now, moving on to some real news, the Entertainment section . . ." After a moment Hope clicks her tongue against her front teeth in disapproval. "Movie stars have it made; another British actor was knighted. What a crock, talk about getting something for nothing. What? The guy can act so now we have to call him Sir?"

"Which actor?"

"The guy who starred in *The King Is Dead*."

"That was a terrible movie."

"You rented it," she says. "Remember?" That was the day Breach called. She shouldn't be anywhere near this conversation.

"Why did that girl call you again?" Hope puts down the paper and looks at me. "Seriously," she says. "Why did she call you? I can't remember."

"I don't know; she was probably bored."

"Do you call her when you're bored?"

"No."

"If she calls again, are you going to tell her to stop?"

"Do you want me to?"

"What's the matter? You like talking to her?"

"It's just the principle, Hope. I mean, I tell you how I feel about you, and you hand me a half-eaten piece of cheese and walk into the bathroom. How am I supposed to know how you're feeling?"

"I'm here, aren't I?"

"Yeah."

"So do you think I'd go spend the weekend with someone I didn't like?"

"I don't know."

"Well you must think highly of me."

"Hope, I think about you all the time. The problem is that I really have no idea if, or what, you think about me."

The exit for our hotel is a mile away. Hope's gaze is fixed on the side of the road. She knows it's her turn to speak.

The hotel is a converted mansion, built a century ago, modeled after a castle somewhere in England. The building is gray and square, with a huge circular driveway, and two bellhops flanking the entrance. Hope walks around the car, opens my door, and stretches into a yawn, then hugs me tight around my neck. A bellhop approaches, "Newlyweds?"

"Not quite," I say. Hope lets go, playfully nudging a shoulder.

"We get a lot of them," he explains.

"I bet," Hope says. "What a beautiful spot."

Before we get a drink Hope wants to unpack. She says she doesn't feel settled until her stuff is put away. I tell her to hurry so we don't miss the sunset and she dumps her bag's entire contents into one drawer. Smiling, she says, "Let's go."

We sit on a patio facing the reservoir. "Look," Hope says, "a lake."

"It's a reservoir. We drove past it."

"Why didn't you tell me?"

"You were a little caught up with current events."

"I'm sorry. I know that was rude. I've been meaning to tell you something but I was waiting until tonight. I almost told you a few nights ago. I knew I wouldn't make it through the car ride if I didn't distract myself."

"Well, can you tell me now, or should I get you a newspaper?"

Hope gives me a look that says "Funny, but not really." Then in a deadpan voice, "I went on the pill. I had to wait a month for it to work. The month is over." She sips her drink looking at me, flicking her eyebrows.

We finished an hour ago but I can't sleep. Hope may be awake too. She said she'd been thinking about the pill for a long time, even before we met. I nodded contemplatively, trying to hide my elation.

Though it's only been an hour, and we haven't really spoken, things have already changed. We've slept with each other now, raising the stakes. And while the words "I love you" are far away, a contract has been drawn to keep us both from leaving.

She stirs slightly and calls my name, her voice slurred and sleepy. She might not even know she's talking. The bed is roomy, a king-size bed, comfortable even with Hope. The pillow's soft too, cradling my neck, elevating my head. It's possible I'm sleeping. Holding my breath, waiting for her to give up, I know I should answer.

"Jack." She speaks a little louder, like she knows I'm awake. "That guy on the street, I *know* what he said."

I roll toward her. "What?"

"He said, *Your* world, not *The*." She curls into a ball and, thankfully, drifts back to sleep before saying another word.

scruples

(seven and a half months later)

Every month when the new fashion magazines come out our living room takes on the appearance of a gynecologist's waiting room. Our coffee table becomes a rainbow of cleavage and capital letters. Hope is smarter than me, there's no doubt. She was just promoted to editor; I still sell ad space. An editor has to know things; a salesman has to smile. A monkey could see these magazines have no substance yet Hope reads them religiously.

Hope's friend, Lelania, enjoys pretending to be a feminist. She tried to be an actress but the farthest she got was a Mentos commercial. She was twenty-two, played a teenager, and didn't have any lines.

Lelania sermonizes to Hope (and anyone else unlucky enough to be in earshot) about the harmfulness of supporting these "oppressive" publications. However, when she visits, their conversation is conducted behind glossy covers, because she's always scouring an article about what men really want in bed.

Last month one magazine had ten of Hollywood's hottest young actors on a cover that folded out like a centerfold.

Lelania spread it across her lap, sighed, and said, "They are all so fucking hot."

"Spoken like a true feminist!" Hope said. When Lelania didn't respond, Hope asked, "Lelania, how is it you can both read and oppose these magazines?"

She looked at Hope like she had asked her how to make toast. "Reading them only strengthens my convictions."

By now her feelings must be pretty strong.

This month's cover displays a prominent Hollywood actress lying down on the pitcher's mound of a baseball field, wearing an evening gown. The ballpark is empty but her hair is perfect. Maybe she got there early. Her cleavage is so airbrushed she appears to be missing some bones in her breastplate. In the lower corner are big red letters saying, "QUIZ: Twenty-five Yes or No questions to find out if HE can be trusted." This magazine has no qualms contributing to millions of eating disorders, but at the same time has devised a simple screening procedure that can detect immorality.

Regardless, a quiz is coming.

That was yesterday afternoon. Thirty-four out of forty points wasn't bad, even if it meant lying my ass off. Hope is happy. She must have called four times today at work.

When I get home from work the phone rings again. This time it's Breach. She's coming to town and wants to get together. Sounds fun to me but obviously Hope will not agree. Breach says something about not being married when the other line clicks. It's Hope's mom. She's sobbing; her dog Slider is dead. The construction workers putting in her new driveway ran the animal over with their steamroller. I offer that it was a quick, painless death, but that doesn't help; in fact, it makes her cry harder. Condolences don't come easy, having never met the dog. Fortunately Hope arrives as I mumble something, rather pathetically, about Dog Heaven.

After Hope has the phone I remember Breach is on the other line. Hope begins to cry too. In her hysterics she might accidentally click back over to Breach. She pulls the phone away from her head, covers one end with her hand and says, "Mom wants to fire the construction company. I don't think that's fair. What should I tell her?"

"It's not gonna help anything, she still has to finish her driveway."

Hope stands motionless, then nods her head firmly once, and talks into the phone. "You need to finish the driveway." She looks at a calendar on the fridge. "The sooner you get construction men out of there, the better. I'll come stay with you until they're done." She listens, then, "No, I doubt he'd be able to leave work on such quick notice." She listens again, her face becoming angry. "That's right, I know, but we're talking about Slider right now, not him." "Him" means me; it's clear by now Hope's mother does not like me which is funny seeing as we've never even met. Hope rolls her eyes at me. "Believe me, Mom, I haven't forgotten our last conversation, or the million other ones before that, OK? I gotta go. I'll call you back later when I know my flight."

It's hard to believe Hope is flying home. Buying a plane ticket seems like an extreme expense to incur just because a dog died. My mother is convinced Hope has money. Hope has never mentioned anything about the subject, but Mom came to her own conclusions judging from Hope's clothes, jewelry, and Mom's strongest evidence: Hope's shoes. When Hope hangs up, the phone rings immediately. She answers and hangs up again.

"That's weird," she says. "Were you on the phone when Mom called?"

"No." For a diversion, "You're going home?"

She interprets the question as a criticism. "My mother's alone, Jack. Death is a bad subject for her. Even if it is just a dog."

"I know. That's not what I meant." Hope stands with all her weight on one leg, her head tilted to that side. She might as well be a snake rattling her tail. "What are you going to tell your boss?"

She shifts her weight to the other leg; the head follows. "I'll tell her I have a family matter."

"That your dog died?"

"No." Her voice becomes stern. "I'll tell her it's a personal problem." Then, quietly, "What she doesn't know won't hurt her."

"That's nice. What don't I know?"

"Sweetheart," Hope walks over and drapes her arms on top of my shoulders. "She's my boss, not my boyfriend."

With Hope gone the first thing to do is get some sugar cereal. I never ate much of it before, but the fact that it's off-limits stirs my appetite. In seven mornings I should be able to finish an entire box.

In the parking lot of the grocery store a car I'd noticed behind me for most of the drive passes up several open parking spaces, turns around and begins to speed up as it approaches. It doesn't slow down and I have to jump out of the way. The car makes a quick turn and exits the parking lot. I don't see the driver but the driver obviously saw me. It's a good thing Hope isn't here; she wouldn't know what to think, and I wouldn't know how to explain.

• • •

The cereal aisle in the supermarket offers an overwhelming selection. Everything looks good. Staring at the rows of animated cardboard boxes I wish someone would come over and make the decision for me. While I struggle, a woman with a baby in her shopping cart checks the price of salad croutons. A scientist somewhere discovered that cereal and croutons placed next to each other increases their chances of being purchased. He's probably the same guy that studies which type of terrible music makes people spend more money.

The woman with the baby holds the croutons and stands still for a second. She's young, maybe twenty, and looks resigned to her haggardness. Something tells me she knows she'll be pushing a baby around for the next twenty years, and isn't thrilled. Her head moves side to side, then she shoves the croutons into a large baby bag slung over her shoulder. While watching the theft in progress our eyes lock so I take whatever box is in front of me and quickly walk away. Not until the register do I notice my choice was granola. Driving to the gym the box sits next to me on the passenger seat. For kicks I buckle it behind the seatbelt.

I'm having a mental affair with Merideth, the woman who introduced herself at my first aerobics class. Hope was right, Merideth is married, and I've seen her with two little kids but I'm pretty sure she's in on the affair too. Merideth and I don't usually speak but she walks by as I'm locking my car. She sees the granola wearing the seatbelt, smiles, and says, "You must really like that stuff." She doesn't slow down or stop to talk.

Sammy and I meet twice a week: Tuesday, to write his ad, and then today, Friday, to see how it looks in the paper. Sammy's got a dictionary on his desk. He's looking up the word

INSIDIOUS, which was written across the bottom of his window last night. All the messages written on the windows are never higher than waist level. Sammy explains, "It's someone tiny writing this stuff. Some kid, you think?" After finding the word he shuts the dictionary and puts it back on a shelf behind him.

I tell Sammy about the dog Slider and he says, "Oh yeah? I knew a guy who got steamrolled once."

"Let's say there was someone I wanted steamrolled, Sammy."

"Who is it?"

"No one really. Just this guy who might be trying to kill me could be my dad."

"Give me his address, I'll get back to you on Tuesday."

I don't answer. His phone starts ringing so I just wave, backing out of his office.

Hope's been gone three days and it's a restless Saturday afternoon. Usually this time is for cleaning our apartment, but that's the farthest thing from my mind. Clean living is good; slacking off's not bad either. The apartment is dusty, cluttered with junk mail and old newspapers; things are out of place. Hope's Magic 8-Ball, her "executive decision maker," has rolled under the kitchen table. The 8-Ball usually doubles as a paperweight, but I'd been playing with it in the living room. Good news: "It is decidedly so" that I'll win the lottery soon.

Someone walks up the steps to our front door. The thought of company is inviting, but the possibility of unwanted company makes me reluctant to answer. Opening the door I'm relieved to see Breach.

I should have smelled her coming. I think she goes

through a bottle of perfume a week. It's a good smell though and when I hug her it sticks to me. She's wearing black pants and a thin, shiny, white button-down shirt. Her hair is still blonde and cut at her shoulders. Her face looks prettier than I remember, which I find troublesome. The mind can be very cruel. She's holding a bottle of red wine.

"Is anyone home?" she asks.

"No," I say. "It's just me. Good timing though. How'd you know?"

"Where is she?"

"She'll be back Wednesday."

While in the kitchen opening wine, I can hear Breach snooping in the living room. When I return with the uncorked bottle, she acknowledges my presence by swiping a finger along a tabletop, then displaying the collected dust.

"Looks like you need to clean house, Jack." She sits on the couch grinning. I sit across from her. We haven't seen each other in over a year, but after ten minutes and a glass of wine, things loosen up.

Drinking in the afternoon makes me giddy. Normally I don't drink wine—I never liked the taste. In this case it's the only thing that makes sense. There's a feeling we're the only two people alive. The world outside Hope's apartment disappears.

When Breach and I split we hadn't cheated on each other, nor had we fought. There were no hard feelings, just mixed ones. Breach looks around Hope's apartment, which I now share with her, and says, "Looks like Jack's all grown up. You were supposed to call me. Remember?"

"I heard through the Drinking Club grapevine you were dating someone."

"Ah. Nothing like the D.C. and their grapevine." She grins.

Breach fills our glasses, kicks her shoes off, and puts her feet up. Then she lies down on her side and props her head up with one hand. The top of her shirt sags a bit, showing part of her bra. She does nothing to cover it. Then she bends forward to grab her wine and gives me a full view. Putting the wine back she pauses, pretending to use extra caution so as not to spill. Hope wouldn't find this so considerate. Breach glances up and catches me looking.

"Jaaaack," she says.

"Yeah?"

"What're you doing?"

I'm feeling the wine. I'm not dizzy but my head is heavy. There's a dull tingle throughout my body. Breach and I used to have the best sex. I love Hope, although I've never told her, and I love sleeping with her, which I'm sure I've mentioned, but I don't think I'll ever experience anything like sex with Breach again. Breach says the same about me, that we've got some strange connection. She says it's chemical.

"Just thinking," I say. "Sorry."

She reaches for her glass and says, "What're you thinking about?" Then pauses again when she puts the glass back. This time I let her watch me stare. Then I look at her eyes. Below them a smirk, above them tilted brows.

"Jack," she says, "come and sit next to me." She rubs circles on the cushion in front of her midsection.

I stand up, not sure if I'm going to sit next to her or pretend to use the bathroom. One definitely sounds better than the other. Just as I'm about to move the phone rings.

"Hello," I say. It's Hope. "How's your mom?" I sound a little drunk, and maybe even horny, if that's possible.

"She's fine. Are you all right? You sound funny."

"No, I'm good."

"What are you doing?"

"I was reading but I kinda fell asleep." Breach follows me into the kitchen.

"Mom and I are going to look at some puppies."

Breach picks up a picture of Hope and points. I nod my head. She grins and puts the picture down.

"That sounds fun."

"You don't understand. We went yesterday, but she started crying before we could get out of the car."

"She misses Slider, huh?"

"I think she feels guilty."

Breach finishes her wine and walks behind me.

"She shouldn't feel guilty." Hope says something back but I miss it because Breach starts to tickle me. Retaliating, I try to whip her with the slack cord of the phone, but instead I catch a basket full of notes and launch it off the kitchen table, sending a shower of miscellaneous papers across the floor.

"Oh! . . . Hello?"

"What are you doing?"

Breach is bent over, stifling her laughter. She writes BATHROOM? on the back of a fallen receipt and hands it to me. I point to the stairs.

"Sorry, the phone fell."

"Did anything break?"

"No. The apartment looks great. You'd be very surprised."

She doesn't say anything and neither do I. It's a long, silent few seconds.

After hanging up the phone I find Breach downstairs. She's in the bedroom looking at Hope's pictures. "Pretty fancy digs, Jack. Hope's cute. A little too preppy for my taste, but I'm sure she's a *smash* at the country club."

"Thanks."

She grabs the Buddha. "I can't believe you still have this."

A little embarrassed, I say, "Why?"

"I figured you threw it out after we decided to take a break. Which reminds me, how long is this break gonna last? I mean shit, Jack, you should go represent a union."

"I like the Buddha."

She laughs. "What was I thinking stealing this thing?"

"You stole it? You told me it came with the drink."

Breach laughs again and covers her mouth with her hand. "I figured you wouldn't want it if you knew I stole it. You're kind of a tight-ass that way."

Insulted, I grab the Buddha and put it back behind the picture of Slider. "I've never been a tight-ass in my life." I step in front of her, pushing my chest out.

Breach looks down at our feet. They're almost touching. She raises her arms like a criminal surrendering, and tilts her head back. Staring down at her neck I'm not sure what to do next. The lace texture of her bra shows through her shirt. The two seconds that pass feel much longer. I put my right hand on her left breast and kiss her neck.

Hope enters my mind and I feel the guilt but stopping's impossible. Kissing Breach again reminds me of the sex. I don't want to cheat (technically) so I keep my blue jeans on. Breach tries to get them off but I won't let her. I can lie if we don't have sex, but I can't have sex and lie.

We fool around for a while then Breach gets up and fixes her hair. She's smiling but it's obvious she feels defeated. At the door she says, "Next time, those jeans are coming off."

With Breach gone I sit on the couch and stare at a picture of Hope and Lelania dressed up as skeletons for a Halloween party. The scent of Breach's perfume still lingers throughout the room. Confessing to Hope is out of the question. She already doesn't like the idea of Breach; this would be the end. Sober, guilty, and anxious about my next conversation with Hope, I need a distraction. Not sleeping with Breach makes things easier on my conscience, but sexually it's frustrating. There's one thing that would alleviate some of the strain but I decide on a workout instead.

Going to the gym is a big mistake. Merideth is there and works out right in front of me, which does nothing to ease my sexual frustration. At the end of class she speaks to me.

"Where's your girlfriend?" She rubs the back of her neck with a towel. Her posture is so nonchalant one would think we've known each other for years.

"She's out of town." Trying to look as casual as her, I rock back on my feet. "How'd you know she was my girlfriend?"

"Educated guess, I guess." She sinks her face into her palms to wipe off her sweat.

I look at her hands. She isn't wearing any rings. "What about you?" I say. "Where's your ring? I thought you were married."

"I am."

"You just don't wear a ring?"

"Nope."

"What's your husband say about that?"

"He ignores it, like everything else."

"Is that the problem?"

"One of them."

"I'm Jack."

"I'm Merideth."

"I know."

She stares at me for a second, then smiles and says, "See you around."

"Uh huh," I say, and almost collapse.

At home I lie on my bed staring up at the ceiling, half expecting it to fall. Breach's perfume is on the sheets; Merideth jump-jacks through my mind, and Hope talks about puppies. I think about my dad. Right now he's hopefully somewhere far away, in a casino, clutching a roulette table, trying to guess where a spinning silver ball will rest. My jackpot will come the day he hits his number and forgets about me. And though there are times I fantasize about getting rid of him myself, the stakes for that kind of gamble are just too high.

The apartment is still a mess. Wayward contents from the fallen basket blemish the kitchen floor. Kneeling, I gather the papers and have to stop myself from ordering them into sleek, configured piles. On top goes the Magic 8-Ball, but first it's polished with a squirt of detergent and a wave of a towel. It almost looks too shiny, and I'm tempted to smear it with fingerprints. From there I move to the counters: a week's worth of dust and a slew of dishes. The floor gets mopped; the fridge pulled out; the cabinets emptied, dusted, and reorganized. For a while it's like I'm not even there.

The living room is next. Furniture is lifted, corners cleared out, windows wiped without a streak. Tabletops and glass-faced picture frames twinkle. Couch pillows are fluffed to angelic proportions. I'm tired and want to sit down, but I'm afraid to disturb it all.

During a final surveillance I find a crumpled piece of paper beneath the hinge of an open door. The receipt with Breach's handwriting.

The garbage bag is fresh and the plastic is still stuck together, so the receipt sort of hovers on top. Exhausted, but restless, I grab it from the trash and rip it into small pieces.

Then I decide to burn them. It feels good so I grab the granola box and light that on fire too. The heat intensifies and I can only hold my hand over it for a few seconds at a time without totally cringing, as the smell of burning hair fills the kitchen. To keep the flame going I grab a newspaper and notice a headline about a local deli going out of business. Not even stopping to read the article I fuel the fire, saying out loud, "Should'a had Sammy on your side, pal," as the paper goes up in flames.

With the ashes down the drain and the stainless steel re-wiped, I wonder how long I can keep this up. Whatever happened with Breach was nothing. I tell myself I'm not married. As for Merideth, there's nothing wrong with flirting. Hope should have never lied to her boss and left town. What you don't know can't hurt you, Hope said. All I need to do is worry about myself, but unfortunately, that's where all the trouble begins.

dominoes

The house is on a piece of land that contains both a forest and a lake. It belongs to the parents of Hope's friend Tianna. The two girls grew up together in Locust Valley, a small suburb on Long Island. Tianna's parents own several homes. They visit this one only two weeks out of the year. A beige gravel driveway snakes through the property. Years ago pine trees were planted along both sides, one after another in two perfect rows, creating a tunnel until the driveway opens into a large cobblestone circle, with a well kept garden in the middle. The circle also accesses a long, narrow parking area laid with the same beige gravel. A high, lush hedge establishes the parking boundary and hides the cars from the house.

Although the house was never a barn it tries to project that image. The bottom half is made with real stone, the top is wood painted red. The roof is curved like a barn's, with green shingles, but the building is stretched too long to have ever been anything but a rich person's dream house. It's a stretch barn. It would look perfect with a limo in the driveway and one of those long, skinny wiener dogs in the yard.

There's a row of rental cars in the parking area. Not the two-door economy jobs, but instead the heavy sedans that old people like. The Continental my delusional aunt left me fits right in. When Hope sees the fleet she says, "Looks like everyone's here." Hope's friends travel every year for Tianna's Fourth of July party. Hope rarely mentions her childhood friends, except to say she doubts I'll like them. My jaw gradually lowered as we drove down the driveway; it dropped completely when we hit the circle.

"Who *are* these people?" I say.

"Don't worry," she says. "Besides, I warned you."

The day Hope warned me we had our first relationship-threatening fight. We were doing volunteer work, putting up a fence around a playground in our neighborhood. Because of the fight, we left before the fence was finished. After Hope's explosion the other volunteers didn't mind.

A convenient stone path from the parking area leads to the front door. The stones match the lower half of the house. The door is propped open, painted red, and split in half horizontally. Both halves are thick and heavy enough to have been their own tree. Hope calls through the screen door but no one answers.

As much as the exterior of the house attempts to look like a barn, the interior does the opposite. The foyer is a two-story room with a retractable roof. The second-floor rooms are joined by a square balcony. A double-wide staircase leads down to a hardwood floor, painted in a green and white checkered pattern. Against the wall to our right is a long, worn, wooden bench. A quilt big enough for a king-size bed is framed on the wall above. Parallel lines of mysterious initials form a pattern. It dates from the nineteenth century. The bench isn't much younger.

"They must be on the porch," Hope says. "Come on."

Hope nonchalantly leads me across the foyer, through a hallway, and into a kitchen. The hardwood floor changes from green and white boxes to light blue. Copper pots hang above a cutting board island. The cabinet and refrigerator doors are glass. The appliances: steel. A red wooden breakfast table, and a red couch and chairs flank either side of the room.

On the porch a bunch of girls sit at a long, white, narrow table. It's cluttered with ashtrays, packs of light cigarettes, Diet Coke, and a few empty wine glasses. Cast off at the end of the table, more for appearance than consumption, is a plate of sandwiches cut into triangles.

The girls, including Hope, are dressed up as forty year olds. They wear their hair back. Tortoise shell headbands seem to be popular, as are sunglasses that make Jackie O's look tame. The shirts have collars and conservative patterns. All skirts are plain but very short, every inch looking expensive. The shoes are as wacky as the sunglasses; apparently accessories are where these girls cut loose. There are two-inch platforms, leopard pattern sandals, two-tone leather saddles, and one girl wears black suede loafers with pineapples embroidered on each foot. All wear men's watches made for deep-sea diving.

The introductions are quick and not awkward. The two names I retain are Tianna, the girl throwing the party, and Grayson, the girl with the pineapple shoes. Hope asks me to go back to the kitchen to get her a Diet Coke. Returning, the girls are huddled around her. It looks like she's whispering instructions. They sit up and change the conversation. At the edge of the porch, I look off toward the lake.

Hope had been acting strange the morning of our fight at the playground. This party put a lot of stress on her. She was nervous about bringing me. I said she could go alone if she wanted. "It's no big deal," she said, "besides . . ." and didn't finish her sentence.

"Besides what?" I said.

"Nothing," she said. "I'm just worried you're gonna think differently about me after you meet my friends and I don't want anything to come between us."

"Well you're in luck. I feel the same way, so I promise not to let your friends influence me."

"I hope it's that simple," she said. "But to tell you the truth, sometimes I feel like I'm living in two different worlds. It can be pretty confusing."

I know all too well what Hope means about living in two different worlds. The other night I staked out Sammy's hoping to catch the mystery marker. I'd been waiting a few hours and it was getting late so I called Hope from a pay phone down the street. When I got back the mystery marker had struck. Written along the bottom of the window was "You're only as good as the company you keep. Shame on YOU! What would your father say."

Because the message was again so low on the window, and the fact that the question mark had been neglected, I started to think Sammy's theory about a kid being the culprit could be right. But when I got back in my car, turned on my headlights, and looked up, I saw the question mark had not been forgotten at all, but instead drawn directly in front of me on my windshield.

Motors rev in the distance off the porch. Tianna walks over and says, "That must be the boys."

"What are they doing?"

"Having a paint ball war. Would you like a drink?"

"What's that sound? It sounds like chain saws."

"Four-wheelers. Makes the game more fun."

Picking up a rifle leaning against the porch railing I say, "Oh, this is a paint gun? It looks so real."

"It is real, Jack."

Looking through the scope magnifies everything and I feel as if I'm floating. In the distance a guy sits on a tree branch looking toward us. He's hard to recognize because the top half of his face is covered by binoculars. He spots me and waves.

"Is it loaded?"

"I don't know, but don't shoot here. We've got a range if you feel like shooting."

"Let's just find out, shall we?" I say, pulling the trigger. The bullet moves in slow motion and by concentrating hard enough I can make it rise or dip, or veer left or right. This is good because having never fired a gun in my life I'm a terrible shot. The bullet makes its way through a few branches and around a tree or two until it finally connects with the target who begins to fall from the tree, also in slow motion. His binoculars drift from his face and for a very quick second I recognize him; he's my friend Mark who should be dead and not in a tree but the second I realize it's him, he vanishes.

From a small break in the woods six guys ride single file on six, red, bouncy-looking four-wheel motorbikes. Five of them are splattered with paint. When Tianna sees them she gets excited and says, "Looks like Alden's the winner!"

Tianna and Alden are getting married at the end of the summer. Their situation is unique in that they were once stepbrother and -sister. Their parents were briefly married when they were younger. After the parents split Alden and Tianna found bliss in the freedom of their ex-step-sibling status. Hope told me this on our way to our volunteer day at the playground.

When the soldiers arrive on the porch they're wearing fresh clothes. Apparently, their paint ball war rations were booze. For some it had been a long, hard battle. The drunkest pounds me on the back, trying to be friendly, and introduces himself as Sonny Wingwright. He asks to be called Sonny, which is fine, although he's twice my size. Insisting on playing pool, he grabs Alden and a guy named Bunny. I'm happy to play. I've never played with anyone named Sonny or Bunny.

The room with the pool table is only for playing pool. Antique-looking stools are placed symmetrically along the walls. Behind a stained wood bar a small glass door refrigerator is filled only with brown and green bottles of beer. The floor is dark-stained wood and almost completely covered by a multicolored, stitched, oval-shaped rug. Hanging on the walls are poster-size pictures of golf course holes, mostly oceanside. Bunny's got a rabbit monogrammed on his shirt pocket. He sees me looking at the pictures. "You like golf, Jack?"

"I don't really play."

He grabs a cigar from Alden and says, "Oh. Well, I guess we'll like you anyway."

"Tianna tells me you work for a newspaper," Alden interjects quickly, trying to cover for Bunny. "How do you like that?"

Sonny is too drunk to get his cigar going so he mashes it in an ashtray. Then he looks at me and says, "How's it living with Hope?"

"She's a great girl," I say.

"Doesn't keep a whole lot of Frosted Flakes in the kitchen, does she?"

Bunny takes the pool cue away from him and says, "Easy Sonny," like he's talking to a growling dog.

Hope's sugar cereal ban was one of the things I asked about when we got in our fight. She was telling me about the people who'd be at the party. She used to date one of them—named Bunny.

"Bunny!" I said. "What kind of a name is that?" She shrugged her shoulders, a little embarrassed. "You grew up with some strange people. That's probably where you got all your weird habits."

We were digging a hole for a fence post. She rested her shovel on the ground and said, "What habits?"

"You know," I said. "No sugar cereal, no turning on the car radio, that stuff."

"Gee Jack," she said. "I never knew you thought I was such an oddball."

Ignoring Sonny, I say, "So Alden, you're getting married soon."

He looks at me as he leans over the pool table, lining up a shot. "Yep. Two months. Bunny too."

Bunny gives me a grave look. I'd forgotten he's marrying Grayson, pineapple feet, the weekend before Alden and Tianna's wedding/family reunion.

"What about you Sonny?" I say.

"Sonny couldn't pick up a hooker with money," Alden says.

I look at Sonny. He's in his late twenties, forty pounds overweight, drunk before sunset, and trying to light the bent cigar.

"Can too," he says, then sticks his head under the bar, resurfacing with a bottle of tequila.

By the time we go back to the porch it's dark; I'm drunk, and smoking a cigar. Alden's my new friend and he wants to ride the four wheelers down to the lake. When asked if Tianna will care, he laughs and says, "Not if I say so." But when we get to the bike shed, which is actually a converted cottage with a loft, he can't find the keys.

"That bitch!" He yells, kicking one of the bikes. "She did it again."

"What?"

"Tianna. She hid the fucking keys."

"She hid them?"

The shed's got a refrigerator, but it doesn't have glass doors. Alden throws me a can of beer from it. "She thinks it's dangerous when we ride the bikes drunk, so she hides the keys."

"Bummer," I say, secretly relieved.

"Do me a favor," he says. "Don't tell her we came down here. She'll get pissed."

"Let me ask you a question." I sit on one of the bikes. "What did Sonny mean when he asked about the Frosted Flakes?"

Alden takes a sip of his beer and decides to finish the can. He walks over, takes two more from the common man's fridge, then sits on the bike next to mine. "You don't know much about Hope, do you?"

"A little. But I'd like to know more."

"Hope's a good person; she'll talk when she's ready. But you're not gonna find anything out tonight; she already told everyone not to talk about her with you."

"Really?" I grab the handlebars of the bike and shake them. "Why would she do that?"

"I don't know. I asked Tianna the same thing. She said Hope must really like you."

Neither of us say anything for a minute. When Alden gets up to go back to the porch, he reminds me not to say anything to Tianna about the bikes.

"What are you hiding?" That's what I had said to Hope that set her off. The whole scene was absurd. We'd just torn down an ugly chain-link fence and were lining up waist-high, colorful boards of wood, painted by children. A beautiful day, surrounded by families, doing volunteer work; I was on a good deed high. I kept asking Hope personal questions even though I knew she didn't want to talk, swept away by the charitable feeling of the day.

Kids were everywhere, some showing off which board they painted. Hope was digging a hole and ignoring me because of my comment about her habits.

"Why is it so wrong to ask what your problem with sugar cereal is?" Looking every bit like a digger, my foot rested on the shovel.

Hope said, "I told you when you moved in, I don't want to talk about it."

Some girls near us played jump rope, chanting easily with the rhythm of the looping cord.

"Well, what about your childhood?" I thought it was an innocent question.

"Will you just help me dig?"

"Sure," I said. "We can talk while we dig."

"Honey, I don't mean to be rude but I just don't feel like talking about it right now."

That's when I should have dropped it but I continued, "What are you hiding?"

She stopped shoveling and stood up very straight. Then she stared at the girls' jump rope like she wanted to turn it into a noose. "Jack," she barked, "we both thought it would be nice to come down here and help out." Her voice was slowly climbing into a shout. "Why do you have to fuck it up by asking me shit I don't want to answer!"

The girls stopped jumping rope. The absence of their chanting made everything seem even more silent. No sounds of shoveling and light chatter. Fuck and shit stopped all action better than any school bell. Everyone was staring at Hope. She looked at me, said, "Jerk," and ran away.

On the way back to the porch the retractable roof in the foyer catches my attention. Pineapple feet finds me wobbling in the middle of the checkered floor, staring up with my head all the way back. "Neat roof," she says.

A little jolted I say, "Grayson, right?" and look at her shoes to make sure.

"It's nice to finally meet you. Hope talks about you all the time."

Still looking at her shoes I say, "Pineapples." It's not a question but it requires a response.

"My mom gave me these. Do you like them?"

"Yeah. Cool."

She looks down and says, "I like them." Then it gets very quiet.

I'm a bad liar when I'm drunk. "Where are you going?" I say.

"To our car to get a sweater." She hooks her arm out and says, "Come with, we'll get acquainted."

Grayson can't remember which rental car is hers, but through trial and error finds her sweater and also a pair of plastic shin guards, which she puts on her legs, fastening them tightly with velcro straps.

Puzzled, I ask, "What's the deal, Pelé?" But Grayson has no idea who Pelé is, and probably thinks the soccer legend's name is actually a high-end facial cream.

"Pelé? Is that Estée Lauder?"

"Close," I say, and point to her shin guards.

"Oh, these?" She chuckles and then explains factually that it's summer and she'll be wearing skirts for most of the season and doesn't want bruises showing up and down her exposed legs. She wears the shin guards when she's drinking because she's been known to "bump" her legs "now and then." I could tell her she could try and drink less, but I think she's quite content wearing shin guards.

On our way back we sit on a bench in the garden so she can smoke. Until now she's been asking questions like where I went to college and where I'm from. Hope probably already told her these things. Then she says, "Hope told me about your fight the other day."

"What'd she say?"

"I don't think you were wrong." She puffs, then, "Of all the years I've known Hope she's never talked to me about her dad. After he died she kept herself a little removed from everyone. It was how she wanted it."

"We weren't fighting about her dad, I was asking about her childhood."

Grayson takes another drag and points her cigarette at me. "That's where you're wrong. Her childhood is all about her dad dying. You asking her about growing up is like asking about her dad."

"So I'm never gonna hear about when she was a kid?"

"She'll tell you. I'm sure she will. She likes you. But Jack, remember, Hope doesn't open up much. So if she does say something, it's a big deal."

"I almost never ask about it."

"I know. I think that's why she likes you so much. The girl's got *a lot* of secrets; between her dad dying and the way her mom totally doesn't cope with it, Hope's got enough baggage for all of us." Grayson takes a final drag then flicks her cigarette into a flower bed.

Back on the porch things have livened up. A hard rock rap song plays from speakers in the ceiling; its got a catchy chorus but the lyrics are all about the singer's trailer trash roots, and though everyone on the porch is enjoying the music, it's safe to assume that this was not the audience the artist envisioned speaking to. Sonny Wingwright is eating, while dancing alone next to the plate of sandwiches. I haven't seen Hope all night and don't want her to know how drunk I am. When she sees me she grabs my hand and starts to dance. She's drunk too. Not too keen on dancing in front of strangers, I let go of Hope's hand and two-step toward the kitchen.

Tianna is by the sink putting ice in a fresh drink. Her back is to me and she's nodding her head to the same song, coming from speakers in the kitchen's ceiling. She sees my reflection in the window but pretends not to notice. Taking a test sip from her glass she begins to sway her hips and move her shoulders in a manner seductive enough to have her arrested in Utah. As she spins my direction her free hand loosens a button on her shirt, while she stares me down, smirking. Then she winks and abruptly heads toward the door, passing Hope on her way out.

"Hey," Hope says to me. "Why'd you come in here?"

"I'm getting a beer."

"Ooh. Get two. Let's go down to the lake."

We make it as far as the bench in the driveway. Hope sits very close to me. She leans her head into my arm.

"Are you having fun?"

"Yeah. Looks like you are too."

"You like my friends?" She twists her head up to look at me and slips off my arm completely.

"Alden's a nice guy. I can't believe he's marrying his step-sister."

"Hhm," it sounds like a laugh. "Pretty straaange. Think we're all strange?"

"No. Sonny's a loser though." Something about the way Hope is acting makes me sit stiffly. She lies down on the bench with her head in my lap.

"You think *I'm* strange." She rolls on her back and looks up at me.

"No I don't," I say.

"Yes you do."

"No. I don't."

"I know you do. You said I have *weird* habits." She sticks her arm up and slaps me lightly on the cheek.

"I didn't mean that, Hope."

"Remember on our first date when you asked about my dad and I told you he died?" She leaves her hand on my cheek. "How come you never asked about him again?"

"You never brought him up."

She starts to pat my cheek again. "Maybe I wanted *you* to bring him up."

I put my hand on the elbow of her arm lying across her chest. "How'd your dad die, Hope?"

She feels for my chin and grabs the bottom of it. "He got held up for his car. They shot him when he got out."

"He got car-jacked?"

"They didn't call it that then. They just called it a robbery."

There's not much more to say than: "I'm sorry. It must have been very hard."

Hope explains, "My mother only let me eat healthy cereal. I was sick the night it happened. He was going to the store to buy me a box of special cereal, to cheer me up."

"Hope, it's not your fault."

"You should have heard me whine, Jack. He didn't want to go against my mom's rules, but finally he gave in just to shut me up."

"Still. It's not your fault."

She shakes my chin gently and says, "I know, but my mother is right. I didn't have to have it, and Dad would have never died."

Hope cries for a while. I sit there and add only my presence. It's enough. When she stops she's much more sober and goes to wash up. I want to ask her what she meant about her mother "being right," but now that she's recovered it seems like a bad idea.

Back on the porch Bunny's rolling a joint. A line of chairs faces the lake. The rapper has been replaced with a female artist who quietly strums a guitar and sings openly lesbian love ballads. Tianna sits in Alden's lap. Next to them, Sonny raises his beer, and says, "Where's Hope?"

"She'll be right out," I say.

Grayson pats the chair next to her, "Come sit, the fireworks are about to start."

In the distance, above town, a white light shoots into the air. When it loses momentum it breaks into smaller lights, cascading until they evaporate. Seconds later we hear its boom. More lights follow: Pinwheels, Flower Pots, and Serpents flare overhead. Each time we hear the explosion late. It strikes me as odd that Hope is missing all this, but when I look over my shoulder, she's leaning on a windowsill, watching, from above.

She waves with one finger, smiles for a second, and looks back up. I follow her lead. We're alike, the two of us. We find our safety not in numbers, but rather in our separateness. Neither superior, nor standoffish, it's the security of self-reliance.

Bunny's joint finds my fingers so I take a hit. The flashes become more frequent. The question mark is still fresh in my mind, written on the clear glass of my car's windshield separating me from the rest of my world.

concentration

Mom wants to talk so she told me to come over Friday night. Her offer sounded like a ploy to get me to serve drinks, but then she explained she had canceled the Drinking Club. I knew I was in for it.

Alice shows anyway. She barely knocks before coming inside. "I founded the damn club, I'll decide if it's canceled or not." She throws her coat on a chair and says, "Jack, how 'bout some wine?"

From the kitchen she and Mom can be heard whispering violently at each other. Finally Mom says, "Fine, maybe you'll come in handy. Just let me do the talking."

I bring out their wine, sit across from them and wait. Mom glances at Alice. Alice says, "Don't look at me, this is your show."

"Jack," Mom says, "I don't quite know how to say this, so I'll just say it. Hope is bad news. I think you should stop seeing her."

"Mom, I live with her. We've gone beyond *seeing* each other."

Alice busts in: "Jack, now is not the time to get caught up in specifics."

Alice has one leg crossed over her knee; she leans back in her chair casually. "You don't like her either?" I ask.

"It's not that I don't like her; I just don't get her. When I lived in New Jersey with my first husband, I knew plenty of women like Hope. They wore designer clothes and ate salads with crab meat for lunch. But this isn't the East Coast, Jack. Look out those windows," she points where to look. "Those are mountains, not Manhattan's skyline."

"So."

"So she's obviously confused. What's she doing out here, if she still acts like she's from New York?"

"First of all, she's from Long Island. And second of all, she came out here to get away from that whole scene, which is one of the reasons I admire her so much. Her mother calls her all the time and gets on her case for being out here."

Mom: "Really?"

"All the time. Her friends too. But Hope sticks to her guns. She doesn't care what anyone says; she likes doing something different."

Mom and Alice look at each other from the corners of their eyes, slightly impressed, but far from being sold.

After celebrating Independence Day at Tianna's, Hope began to change. A difference was noticeable the second we got in the Continental to drive home, her friends' rental cars still in our rearview mirror.

"Jack," she said, "you know I'm doomed."

The car had reached the entrance of Tianna's impressively long driveway. "How's that?"

"Because I've seen my future, and it doesn't look good."

"How 'bout mine?"

"Jack, I'm being serious. Every single one of those girls

asked me when I planned to move home. It's like they're all laughing at me because they know that sooner or later I'll be back. My mother sends me the real estate section every week. She circles the apartments she thinks I'll like."

"That's a little much, but at least you know she wants you around."

"To be honest, my mother and I are better off if we're not together. She tries to control my life, and I try to get back at her. Like one time she set me up on a date without telling me. She had this guy come to our house and pick me up, but she never even mentioned he was coming."

"That's crazy. Did you know him?"

"Sort of. His name was Baldwin; he's a few years older than me. My mom is friends with his mom. When he finished law school, Mom said, 'Send him over. Hopey's free.'"

"How was the date?"

"I probably shouldn't even tell you."

"Too late. Once you start something, you're not allowed to stop."

At the highway access ramp there was a gas station, a western bar with a wooden painted sign advertising homemade chili, and a drug store with a neon beer sign blinking in the window. The traffic light was red.

"OK, I'll tell you," Hope said, "but promise you won't make fun of me."

"Well I can't do that, but I promise to try not to."

"Good enough. First of all, you have to understand that this guy was such a loser. He thought he was like Johnny Lawyer, or something. He wore these wire-framed glasses and his hair was all slicked. Driving us to the restaurant he called his home phone from his cell phone to see if anyone at work had called. He apologized, explaining he was in the middle of a *big* case."

"This is who your mom wants you to date?"

Sarcastically: "He's perfect. A lawyer. From Locust Valley. Come on."

"So what did you do?"

The traffic light turned green and a hundred yards later we were on the highway traveling east, Tianna's compound and the homemade chili quickly fading behind us.

"He took me to this restaurant, which is also kind of like a bar. Everyone goes there. It's like the Cheers of Locust Valley. So Tianna and Grayson, and all those guys are there just watching me squirm."

"I love it."

"I know. It was totally embarrassing." Hope chuckled. "So Johnny Lawyer and I ran out of things to talk about after 'Hello,' right?"

"Was he at least a good-looking guy?"

"Actually, yes. He was pretty hot, but listen. He started talking about politics, and he went off on this long rant against gay rights."

"And that's when you fell in love?"

Hope laughed. "Not quite. I got Tianna, and we concocted a little scheme in the ladies' room."

"Did you T.P. his car?"

"Better. We made out in front of him."

"What!?!"

"Do you love it?"

"I don't believe you."

"I swear to God. It was Tianna's idea. She walked back to the table with me and said, 'Baldwin, Hope and I have a secret . . . We're lovers.' Then she planted one on me. You should have seen the look on his face, it was priceless. He got out of there pretty quick after that."

"So what was it like kissing Tianna?" I flicked my eyebrows and grinned.

"It was nothing. We had planned the whole thing out, so I knew it was coming." Hope reached forward and turned on the car stereo. "How's the sound system in this tank, anyway?"

Mom and Alice go into hysterics. "That's classic," Alice says. "Talk about Girl Power!"

Mom reaches over and grabs Alice's knee. "Baldwin, Protector of The Straight World!"

Alice asks, "Did her mother ever find out?" Both women hush.

"The very next day," I say. "Hope woke up to find her bags packed and her vacation cut short. Her mother kept her locked in an insane asylum for the next four months."

"Jesus," is all even Alice can say.

"According to Hope, her mom lost any soul she might have had when Hope's dad died."

Both women get quiet again so I go to the kitchen for more wine and a bottle of beer. Mom calls from the living room, "Jack, how are you going to compete with guys named *Baldwin*?"

Alice shouts, "Maybe you should change your name to *Jacques*."

That night, when we got home from Tianna's, Hope brought out a stack of picture albums. She said she wanted to explain how she could see her future. Her argument was convincing, and it seemed like she had arranged her pictures in an order to prove her case.

The first book began with class pictures from kindergarten through twelfth grade. Hope went to an all girls' school. In photo after photo, for thirteen consecutive years, she stood amidst a tight row of girls wearing the same uniform, a blue dress to the knee line and a white-collared shirt.

"I can't believe you had to wear a uniform to school," I said.

"Yeah, they really let us think for ourselves."

In the summer, for a large portion of those thirteen years, Hope went to a day camp where she also had to wear a uniform—white shorts and a plain white shirt. The girls had pigtails and the boys had bowl cuts. Most everyone was blond. At the back of the book were some black-and-white pictures from her mother's years. Same school, same uniform. They even had the same second grade teacher.

Another book was full of pictures taken every year at a Labor Day party where people gathered on a lawn in front of an old windmill. The album had a green leather cover. "Windmill Party" was engraved in the bottom right-hand corner.

Hope said, "Look closely."

She had ordered the pictures from Past to Present, coupling her friends next to her friends' parents. Every year the two groups started to look more and more the same. In the last picture, Grayson was wearing the same sundress as Tianna's mother; a sleeveless blue number, speckled with seashells.

Hope rolled her eyes and said, "It created *quite* the stir." Then she flipped the pages back almost to the beginning, pointed to a man, and said, "That's my father."

I looked closely.

"I'm surprised I never showed you these before. I must have been saving them for the right moment."

"I'd like to see more," I said.

She leaned over, kissed me, and opened a thin book spotted with pictures only of her father. She started off telling the story behind each photograph, but about halfway through got too upset, so she just turned the pages.

Alice wants to know, "Was he handsome?"

"Yeah. And I'll say this too, Hope's parents really looked like they were in love. There wasn't one picture where they weren't holding hands or touching in some kind of way."

"Gee Jack, sounds like a pretty fancy crowd. Where do you see yourself fitting in?" Mom looks to Alice for support of her question.

"Hope might have money," I say, "but a lot of people see that as a good thing. Right, Alice?"

Alice looks at Mom and shrugs. "Never stopped me."

Mom tries to bully Alice back to her side by saying, "Tell me one thing that's *ever* stopped you, Alice."

Alice grins tightly, looks at me, then at Mom, and with a much quieter, almost demure voice says, "You mean besides bad sex?"

Hope showed me a picture of Baldwin taken at a Christmas party hosted by her mother. He stood in between his mother and Hope's mom. The picture was only a year old. He was handsome, which is probably the best word to also describe the two older women he politely had his arms around, who looked almost identical except for the arch in Hope's mother's left eyebrow, which in Eyebrow language said, *Put the camera down, Hope.*

Hope closed the book and said, "It just struck me that we share this apartment and you don't even have any pictures of your own up. I can't believe I've been so rude."

"I really don't have many pictures, not anything worth framing at least."

"No?"

"I have some funny pictures of me and my friends from college, but they look better in a shoe box, if you know what I mean."

"But your mother is so pretty. You must have a picture of the two of you."

"I'll check next time I'm over there."

"She really said that?" Mom slides forward in her chair. "Were you two drinking?"

"No, Mom. We were just hanging out. That's one of the best things about Hope: she can actually be really easy to be with."

Mom and Alice look at each other, then both sip their wine.

So I continue: "I know, she's got a temper, and she can be a bit irrational, but she's human. Everybody gets upset."

Alice can't hold it in but manages to spit her wine back into her glass before laughing, coughing, and laughing again. Mom pinches her nose.

I maintain a serious expression that reins them in.

"Okay fine," Alice says, "But what do you guys talk about? I have a hard time seeing what you have in common."

"Have in common? We live together. We share a newspaper in the morning, cook dinner at night, we went to the same college, we're the same age. What do you think we talk about?"

Alice doesn't blink. "I haven't the slightest. Why weren't you friends in college?"

"Alice, there were twenty-five thousand other students. We just didn't cross paths."

"Fine, Jack, you win. You and Hope are *perfect* for each other."

"Thanks, Alice."

Alice lifts her glass. "Here's to a match made in heaven."

"What do you know about heaven?"

Mom interrupts. "That's enough. Both of you."

Alice looks at me and nods a silent apology.

"Sorry, Alice," I say back. "I'm sure you know a lot about heaven."

"It's okay, Jack." Alice can't stop smirking.

"Like who to sleep with to get there."

Mom erupts. "Alright, Jack, if you're gonna get smart then I guess I have to map things out for you. Alice is absolutely right. You're not thinking about the long term at all. You and Hope can hang out and look at pictures until your eyes fall out, but eventually she's gonna want to get married and spend the rest of her life with someone and you guys would be a lot better off if you had more in common than the daily news and a mutual acceptance of how long you boil your pasta."

That requires some silence, but after a minute I say, "Well, if Hope is as loaded as you guys think, marrying her might not be such a bad idea. Why not take a chance and live a little, right? Being rich and unhappily married can't be any worse than poor and single. It might even be better."

"Jack," Mom says, "you've got your whole life ahead of you. You don't have to worry about being poor and single yet."

"Exactly. If things don't work with Hope, I'll have plenty of time. But if she's *so* wealthy that we have nothing in common, it might be worth the risk just to see another side of life."

Mom doesn't like this. She puts down her wine glass and sighs. "Let's keep it so your father's the only gambler in the family. Please. Besides, I can't imagine what kind of scheme he'd try and pull if he found out you married into money. But I can promise you this much, he'd definitely be back in your life."

Mom doesn't know about Dad's recent antics. It would only upset her and I'd like to think his efforts are harmless.

"Mom, I'm just kidding. Hope and I have never even talked about getting married. I don't even know how this conversation got started."

Alice chimes in: "Because your mother and I were telling you that in the long run, you and Hope won't float, capisce?"

"Well maybe I'm not such a believer in the long run. I don't think Mark spent the last day of his life shoveling gravel because he knew he was gonna die that afternoon. Okay?"

Both women moan, more frustrated than sympathetic.

There were two pictures in the back of Hope's final album. One was of herself when she was very young, standing in the middle of an ice rink wearing figure skates, white tights, and a matching outfit bejeweled with silver sequins. Hope covered the picture with her hand and said, "Don't look at that."

Two of the greatest things about our town are the view of the mountains, and the mad swings of weather. In January it can snow a foot one day, and be sixty-five degrees and sunny the next. It was on one of these warm, sunny days, shortly following a major snowfall that the second picture was taken. The image was of Hope, wearing boots, shorts, and a sweater, standing at the foot of the mountains with her hands on her hips. She was smiling, but her mouth was closed, and really, she simply looked determined.

Mom walks me to my car. She watches me buckle my seat belt and says, "It was a terrible thing, what happened to Mark. But it's no reason for you to quit thinking about your future, or Hope's for that matter."

"I know, Mom, but right now I'd rather just concentrate on the present. Believe me, I have enough on my mind already."

"You know Breach was here last Friday night. I think she had a little too much to drink because she had a lot to say about the two of you."

Trying to sound surprised I say, "Really?" Lately Breach and I have been keeping in touch. She'll call me at work every once in a while or send me a funny email. It's nice and we both seem to understand there's a boundary we can't cross.

Mom leans into the car window right as I'm about to back up, "Jack, I'm not claiming to know everything about what's going on in your life, but if you even think there's a remote chance you might some day want to end up with Breach you should be honest about it with Hope, and yourself for that matter."

"I appreciate the fact you think Breach and I are a good match, but it's a little more complicated than that."

There are times I think about Breach and I getting back together and it's tempting to say the least, but the funny thing is it's not Hope's feelings I worry about. What I find most troubling about the prospect of reuniting with Breach is the potential of us hurting each other all over again. I don't care how perfect we are for each other; things rarely ever work out according to plan.

Mom steps back from the car, shrugs her shoulders and says, "Drive carefully."

I leave with no pictures. They were all warped and dusted, and the only good one of Mom and me had tack holes in each corner.

Hope is gone when I get home, but leaves a note asking me to meet her at her friend's house. Written below her name is OPEN, with an arrow pointing at a box wrapped in blue and white paper. Inside are two picture frames. One is silver and has a picture of Hope and me at Tianna's Fourth of July party. The other frame is faded wood, and empty. Stuck to the glass is a note that says, "I think this will go well in the living room. Did you find anything at your mother's?"

clue

It's truly a magnificent bathroom. The mirror alone is special—a family heirloom no doubt. Concave in shape, it reflects any angle. Hope swears it's a "skinny mirror," that all the mirrors in Tianna's house are biased. A distorted portrait perhaps, but I've never seen myself look better.

Nubility looms in the final, dwindling days of summer here in Locust Valley, Long Island, for back-to-back weekends of matrimony. Bunny and Grayson paired off last night, but they're waiting for Alden and Tianna to start the honeymoon. The two couples should've had a joint wedding. They're using the same church, same club for the reception, same guests, and probably the same menu too. Supposedly a joint wedding is "tacky."

Hope is Tianna's maid of honor. We're staying with her and Alden until the big day. Hope grew up somewhere around here but we haven't been by her house. If it's anywhere near Alden and Tianna's neighborhood, I'd be very interested to visit.

Two of my best friends live in New York City. They moved to become businessmen, enticed by exotic phrases like *risk arbitrage* and *leverage buyouts*. Christmas was the last time they came home. Talked to both on the phone but will see neither.

Hope's got this entire week planned out, my friends excluded. Doesn't matter though, we've been tight fifteen years; nothing's come between us.

In an honest moment Hope told me her mother does not and will not ever like me. Very bluntly Hope explained I am from the "wrong type" of background, and however embarrassing it is for Hope to admit, her mother is her mother and there's nothing she can do. Hope had said, "Believe me Jack, I'm not proud of it, but for whatever reason, Mom feels she's entitled to act any way she wants, and if I could change her, I would. Just be warned, and if she says or does anything out of line, let me be the first to apologize now, before it even happens because I know something will."

I meet Hope's mother for the first time over lunch. The restaurant is congested with malnourished but heavily jeweled, tan women, sipping iced teas and nibbling on bread. The better-looking ones brave the air-conditioning, keeping their blazers off to display their arms, bracelets, and hardened nipples. Hope walks up to an attractive one, guilty of such self-promotion. She greets Hope with a hug, then turns to my extended arm saying, "You're not getting away with just a handshake," air-kissing both sides of my face while putting an arm around my waist. Before she unlatches she gently squeezes my hip a few times saying, "Well this should be fun," then winks at Hope.

The two women share a salad. They pick at it together as her mother navigates my life story. Hope must have told her about my father because he's the only topic she avoids. Obviously she wants to keep things light.

"So how about all these weddings?" She says, wrapping up my segment of the lunch.

"I know," Hope says, "it's so exciting."

"What do you think, Jack?" Her mother asks.

Hope also prepped me before lunch. Her mother doesn't approve of Alden and Tianna's marriage. Ex-step-siblings should not be husband and wife. She's got a point. "It's great," I say. "I mean, they're young, but if they're in love why stop them?"

Hope's mom juts her nipples forward and says, "I just think it's fantastic. And the fact that the in-laws were once married is so sui generis." She raises her eyebrows. The false sincerity in her voice probably hurts Hope the most.

"It certainly is unique," Hope says.

"What about you two? Any big announcements?" She directs the question at no one in particular, but Hope doesn't answer, waiting for my response. It feels as if everyone in the restaurant has stopped talking to hear my answer.

"I doubt it," I say. "I don't see any point in rushing."

They sit back. If the three of us were playing poker, I'd fold.

"You never know." Hope's mom sighs nostalgically. "When Hope's father proposed, he didn't know what he was doing. We were stopped at a traffic light, on our way to see a show in Manhattan. An old man on the corner was waiting for a bus. He was sitting on a bench, reading a newspaper in the dark. While we waited a bus arrived, but he didn't get on. Hope's father stared at him until the light turned green. Halfway down the block he asked me to marry him."

Hope says: "Who says I want to marry Jack in the first place?"

"Well, if history repeats itself, you won't be too far behind your friends." Hope's mother quickly looks in my direction. "No need to rush."

Hope lifts my hand from the table and kisses it, her eyes

never leaving her mother's. "But of course, mother dear. But of course."

Hope holds my hand for the remainder of lunch until she excuses herself to the ladies' room. Once Hope has left, her mother grabs my same hand and says, "Let me keep this warm until my daughter gets back." Because I know the woman doesn't like me, I let her, thinking maybe this display of affection is her way of saying I'm okay. Unfortunately, very little time passes until I'm forced to excuse myself to the men's room upon feeling her thumb glide back and forth across the full width of my palm.

Alden and Tianna live in the same house their parents lived in when they were married. Tianna's mom got the house from the divorce. When she remarried she gave it to Tianna. It's a big house. Guests fill every room this week, but right now everyone is out. Alden, Bunny, Sonny, and I enjoy a beer in peace.

Tianna is waiting until after the wedding to play house. Currently the decorations and furniture span from the Fifties up through the Nineties. The table in the kitchen has folding metal legs and a lime-green top, matching the accompanying chairs' built-in, plastic padding. On top of the table are scented candles and a ceramic bowl bought recently at a furniture outlet. Two cream-colored, ceramic containers have a monkey wearing a disco outfit painted on the front. One groovy monkey covers his ears. The other covers his mouth. The "see no evil" must have broken. Hanging on the stove door are new, green dishtowels. A pink whale, spouting water above the date, 1892, is sewn at the bottom.

"What's up with the whale?" I ask Alden.

"Those are from our club, GreadeRock." He grabs one and wipes his bottle of beer.

"GreadeRock?"

"I know," Alden looks at the whale on the towel. "It's a terrible name but all the land was donated by some guy named Laddo Greade when he died."

"How'd he die?"

"Consumption."

"What kind of club?"

He pauses, thinking about how to describe it.

Bunny jumps in. "It's got everything: golf, tennis, beach, and there's this place to eat called The Pit that's right next to the pool. The food is really greasy, perfect for a hangover."

All three nod.

"It's got a great golf course," Alden says.

"Good drinks too," Wingwright adds. "We're joining when we're thirty." Sonny grabs the towel from Alden and tends to his bottle.

The new bride, the bride to be, and Hope are in town. Bunny seems no different now that he's married; Alden shows no acknowledgment of his own imminent nuptials. The honeymoon is a hot topic however; both boys are looking forward to taking a trip together. The deal with the wives allows golf five of the ten days. They're conspiring to play a straight week. This leads to a conversation about other trips the four have taken together—romance sired by eighteen holes for the boys, beach chairs for the girls, and a lot of cocktails for everyone at night.

"So how'd you guys know when to get married?" I ask.

They look at each other and shrug. Bunny says, "I don't know. Just kind of knew. You know?"

I take a moment to wonder if all guys named Bunny are as bright as he, before I ask, "What about you, Alden?"

He takes a deep breath, looking to the side, and squinting. "It was more Tianna's idea than mine. One night she was just kind of like, 'So when're we getting married?' and I said, 'Whenever you want.'"

"Seriously?"

Bunny nods, then Alden continues. "Well it wasn't that simple, but I knew we'd break up if I didn't do something. We were living together already. If we broke up, I'd have to move out; besides, I love her."

"He had it easy," Bunny says. "One night, out of the blue, Grayson said I had five minutes to decide if I wanted to spend the rest of my life with her."

"And you said yes?"

"Yeah. Alden had just asked Tianna to marry him. I figured if he could do it, so could I."

Sonny gulps down the remaining half of his beer, burps to get his breath and says, "I'd do it."

Alden's father appears at the kitchen door. He's a short man who carries himself with great importance. He ignores me because he's never seen me before. Supposedly he's a famous businessman, but I've never heard of him. My friends in New York were impressed I'd be at his son's wedding. Hope says he's mean to Alden. Bunny's kissing his ass.

My dad sent me a letter recently. He asked how my job was and if there was anything exciting going on in my life. Did I have a girlfriend? If yes, what was she like? He said he missed me. He begged for forgiveness. All he wanted was an amicable relationship. He included an address, but I didn't write him back. I just wanted to know how he got my new address.

When Bunny finally loosens his nose from the backside of Alden's father, Alden and his dad go talk in another room.

"That looks pretty serious," I say.

"Nah," Bunny says. "He's probably just making sure Alden isn't getting cold feet."

"Fatherly advice, eh?"

Sonny smirks and says, "You could call it that."

"That's good," I say.

"Yeah," Bunny says. "Tianna owns five percent of his company, thanks to her mom. He wants it back in the family."

"Alden knows this?" I ask.

With the GreadeRock towel Bunny wipes a circle of water left from his bottle of beer. "It's all he's heard about from the moment they started dating."

Alden comes back into the kitchen. His dad left through the front door. "I gotta go to the hardware store," he says. "Dad wants me to buy some new hoses for the house."

As the three leave, Alden's brother, Adrian, arrives. A taxi drops him off. No one had ever mentioned his existence. Adrian is taller, gaunt, and obviously gay. He's got brown hair that's cut very short, a tight goatee on his chin. He's wearing a white T-shirt that probably cost forty bucks, tucked into a pressed pair of khaki pants cinched high and tight around a small waist. The shoes look Dutch or German. His movements are cautious and faint. The brothers shake hands. Adrian understands Alden must do their father's errand.

Inside, Adrian looks around the kitchen with a smirk on his face. The candles and bowl from the furniture outlet make his lips quiver. He looks at the monkey containers like they've insulted him. The GreadeRock towels send a laugh through his nose.

"I can't believe he'd actually put these rags in his house,"
he says, holding up the pink whale.

"I think he likes them," I say.

"What's your name again?"

"Jack. I'm here with Hope."

He thinks a second and says, "I always liked Hope. She's
got a little more substance than the rest of them. Now let me
tell you about this place," he flutters the towel. "Dinosaurs
didn't go extinct. They became alcoholics and signed up at
GreadeRock." He smiles. "No, actually it's worse than that.
Picture the dinosaurs wearing madras clothing, straw hats,
and gaudy accessories with a bunch of Hitler Youth running
around. That's GreadeRock."

"Sonny says they make good drinks." I smile to make sure
he knows I'm not serious.

He laughs and says, "He'd be the one to know. Yes, Sonny
likes them stiff, like the people."

"So where do you live?" I ask.

"In Manhattan." He pours himself a glass of wine.

"What do you do?"

"I'm a graphic designer." He takes a quick sip.

"What do you design?"

"Well," he says, tapping his foot lightly, "right now I'm
doing three-dimensional work."

"You mean like sculptures?"

"No." He chuckles. "Although I have seen some very
graphic sculptures. Here, let me show you."

Adrian pulls a calendar-sized notebook from his briefcase.
The pad is full with drawings of different colored lines that
look like a pattern, but when seen from just the right sight-
line, a figure surfaces, usually of a spaceship or a galaxy.

He turns to a dizzying page of blue and purple lines, and

tells me to find a waterfall. "The trick is not to look too closely," he says. "Try standing back."

Doing what he says doesn't help. The waterfall never shows. He leaves the page open, and leans it against the wall. "Don't think about it anymore," he says. "Glance at it from time to time, maybe it'll appear in a flash."

We're silent for a minute, making us both uncomfortable. He breaks it with, "So, Alden's marrying our old stepsister. How *avant-guard*."

"You're the first person who's said something," I say.

"I left this scene a long time ago. I see things they either can't or choose not to." The phone rings. Adrian answers with a wink, "Hotel New Hampshire, how may I direct your call?"

It's the girls. Their car battery died. Alden took the other car to get his hose. Tianna says to borrow the neighbor Mr. Hornblower's car. He's a friend and won't mind. The directions she gives are mostly landmarks because she doesn't know any of the roads' names.

"Don't you live here?" I say.

"Exactly," she says. "What do I need to know the names of the roads for?" Then she says in a playfully sinful tone, "I'll give you a tour later sweetheart. Locust Valley has a lot of nooks and crannies; it's an easy place for a visitor to lose his way."

Tianna started flirting with me the day Hope and I arrived. She's obviously trying to cram some last minute fun in before her wedding and being an outsider makes me a perfect mark because who would I tell? And more important, who would believe me? There's no real intent behind her words; she's always saying things with a smirk.

"I don't know," I say, perpetuating the charade, "why

would I want a tour from someone who doesn't even know the names of the roads? I mean, how good could that be?"

"Jack honey, don't let yourself get caught up in all the details; besides, it's the lay of the land that's so impressive." Then in a confident, almost humorless voice, "You'll see."

Mr. Hornblower answers the door wearing frayed madras shorts and a yellow collared shirt with a blue GreadeRock whale on the left breast. The fossil of a man who probably once rowed crew at an Ivy league school, his legs are too skinny to support his tall frame, so he stands with a hunch, hands shoved in back pockets. His loafers are shiny, but very worn. No socks.

Hornblower elects to drive me into town. A drive would be nice; besides, he isn't busy.

His car is an old station wagon with fake wood lining. He's aware the passenger window doesn't roll down. It isn't often he has passengers, so fixing it's not a priority. The front seat is faded, blue plastic material meant to look like leather. The dashboard is dusty; a few pennies are wedged at the corners of the windshield.

"Thanks again for driving me," I say.

"Not a problem." He's got a throaty, almost British accent. "I don't mind helping out Tianna. I watched her grow up. Hard to believe the gal's getting married."

"She and Alden are both very happy," I say.

"What a gas! Who'd have thought those two would end up together? Great, isn't it?"

"Are your kids married?"

"No. Don't have children." One thing about Hornblower, he's a good driver. The roads are thin and curvy, lined with thick trees and stonewalls. He keeps a steady hand, accelerating through even the blind turns. "I never got married," he says, "so I didn't have to think about children."

When we get to the brides and Hope, Mr. Hornblower buys a box of crackers and a block of cheese at a newsstand. He waits with us, then follows us home. From his front door he waves a last time, before going inside with his dinner.

The rehearsal dinner is tonight. Having showered first, I wait in coat and tie, on a bed which is too soft not to have been a Fifties leftover. Hope's in the bathroom, wearing a skirt and bra around her waist, doing something to her face and hair. She talks to my reflection in the mirror, through the open bathroom door. Tonight she'll be sitting at a different table but managed to get me seated with Adrian.

"That reminds me," I say, getting up and leaning slightly into the bathroom so she can hear me whisper. "You never told me Alden has a gay brother."

"Who?" Her hands freeze by her ears. "Adrian?"

I lean in further and say, "Like you didn't know."

She makes her hands busy again. "You're out of your mind."

"I like him," I say. "He's just gay, that's all."

"Jack. I've known these people longer than you. I think I'd know if one of them was gay."

"Maybe not."

Hope quits her business in the bathroom and comes to stand over me. "I wouldn't go *rushing* to any conclusions," she says. "Seeing as you think it's a bad idea to *rush,* and all."

"What? Are you mad at me now?" Instead of responding she shimmies her bra up, over her breasts. "Is this about lunch?" I ask. "Because if it is, you really should give me a break. How was I supposed to know what to say?"

"I don't know, Jack. How were you?" She goes back into the bathroom and shuts the door.

Adrian is a welcome dinner partner after the episode with Hope. Eventually she did come out of the bathroom. She apologized, explaining that being home, especially near her mother, put a lot of pressure on her. Her peace offering was heartfelt; she still hadn't put on a shirt. Talking with Adrian is fun; he's a smart guy. He speaks of his work like it's a family member. Earlier he waved to his father, but I'm not sure if they've actually spoken yet.

The chatter in the room is reserved. Conversations grumble and murmur with the slow, deep sounds of an upset stomach. Sitting at our table are Missy and Bo Shiverick, a terse pair who've said about as little as they've smiled. To their left is a rather solemn couple named Kitty and Richard Cheswick. Richard sits like he's got a two-by-four for a spine and he's as animated as a lighthouse at noon. His face should show an expression any minute. Wine gets the best of Kitty. After two glasses she slumps forward, and talks only about her husband's commercial real estate business. On Missy and Bo's right are Rick Major and his date, Miranda Greenleaf. Rick's a thinker. About what, no one knows. Miranda's a talker though, a loud talker, loud enough for everyone at the table. After wincing smiles through twenty minutes of drivel about which boarding school her children are applying to, we manage to escape outside.

"Fun group," Adrian says, handing over a cigarette. "I hope your friends are more exciting."

"I love my friends," I say. "Same guys since seventh grade."

"Wow. You still see them a lot?"

"Not really. Two live in New York, the other two in California."

"So who do you hang out with?"

It takes a minute but eventually it's clear that I have no answer. Mark would have never moved had he not died. The gang that Breach and I hung with are still around, but she got to keep them after we split.

Inside, Alden, Bunny, Tianna, Grayson, Sonny, and Hope are standing at the bar. Hope sees me walking in with Adrian and raises her eyebrows suggestively, smiling.

At home in our bedroom Hope is worn out. She made a good speech at dinner and is proud of herself. She'd sat with me afterwards, saying I was the only person who could calm her nerves. Her back faces my side of the bed.

"Hey," I say lying down next to her, "you going to sleep already?"

"The wedding's tomorrow. I gotta rest."

"Come on," I say, shaking her shoulder. "We barely talked tonight. Sorry about our fight."

"I'm sorry too." She rolls onto her back. "It's just weird. Being here, seeing my friends get married. I can't help but wonder."

"You're gonna get married, Hope." Giving her knee a few quick squeezes I say, "I hear Sonny Wingwright's available."

"Not funny."

Leaning down to kiss her, I say, "You know I'm joking."

"Get away from me." She turns her head.

"Come on. I was kidding."

She rolls back over and says, "It's okay Jack, really. Let's just go to bed."

"Hope. I'm sorry. I was trying to be funny."

"Don't worry about it. I just want to sleep."

With some force I'm able to turn her toward me. "I'm sorry," I say. "I was playing."

She kisses me back for abatement only. When I try for more she says, "Not tonight, Jack. Besides, you wouldn't want to get me pregnant. You might have to marry me."

A debate about abortion seems inappropriate, so I let it go at that.

Bunny and Sonny are in the kitchen the next morning. Tuxes wrapped in plastic bags hang off the back of a chair. I've never had to deal with the boys this early in the morning, but fortunately hangovers keep them quiet. The sight of Alden gives them a jolt though, and their animated exchanges make me miss my friends. Not an entirely foreign sensation, but the capricious schedule it keeps is what's unsettling. Of late, Hope has helped. As I listen to the three boys, I can't help but look over my shoulder to see if Hope is near. I sneak upstairs, and surprise the girl, who by herself, has filled my loneliness.

When I get to our room it's empty except for a growing layer of steam, spreading across the ceiling from a crack in the bathroom door. Hope is humming "Here Comes the Bride," not suspecting my proximity. Waiting, I act out different approaches. She turns the shower off and curses.

"What is it?" I say.

"Jack?"

"I came to visit."

"There's no towel in here, will you bring me one?"

I hold the towel open with both arms. She smiles, stepping into my offering backwards. "I missed you," I say, helping her rub the towel against her skin. "And I forgot to tell you something."

"Yeah?"

"I love you."

She turns and embraces me, the towel stays pinched between us. Her arms are wet and warm and stick to my shoulders instantly. Buried in the moist tangle of her hair, my nose itches, but what's more overpowering is her shampoo's mango scent. Inhaling, I squeeze her tighter and hold my breath.

"You smell good," I say, and step away from her.

The wedding goes off without a hitch. Adrian and I sit together toward the back. Mr. Hornblower comes in late, and sits alone, behind us.

risk

My mental affair with Merideth, the woman from aerobics, has gained momentum. It didn't take long for Sammy to notice. We were in his office a few weeks ago, the windows had said, YOUR WORLD IS COMING TO and nothing else. Somehow Sammy had ended up with a tremendous inventory of potato chips. Boxes were piled everywhere. He wanted his ad to say, Roses are red, violets are blue, free chips with any sandwich, because Sammy loves you. I told him that was fine, but when he looked at the draft, I had written the wrong dates.

"Jack, what'sa matter? You don't know what month it is?"

I looked at the paper and saw my mistake. "Oy. This woman is driving me crazy."

"Hope? She's your girlfriend, she's supposed to."

"Not her."

"Oh." Sammy grabbed the ad form and fixed the dates himself. "Who?"

"This woman from my gym, Merideth."

"Woman? How old is she?"

"Thirty-something? I don't know. She's gorgeous, Sammy, I mean drop-dead. Blonde, blue eyes, they couldn't design a better looking woman if they tried."

"Yeah sure, but *thirty-something?* Isn't that a little out of your range, kiddo?" Sammy pulled a bag of chips from a box behind his desk and offered me one.

"No, that's actually what draws me to her. She's been around longer than me so naturally she knows more. She seems together, you know? Like her life is normal and she's got a handle on it. I don't know many people like that. I bet she gives really good advice."

Sammy's grin said he wasn't buying it. But then, with an almost tender nostalgia, he spoke of guilt and opportunity, weighing both against the undisputable fact that a person only lives once. Then he said, "Ask her out for coffee. What all can happen over a cup of coffee?"

Before Hope and I departed for the wedding safari in Locust Valley, I'd decided to approach Merideth at aerobics. Hanging on the wall behind her were posters autographed by local athletes who train at our gym.

"Would you like to go for coffee?" It was that easy.

She crossed her arms and in an accusatory tone asked, "Why are you doing this?"

"You seem like a nice person."

"Hardly a reason."

"Well, do you want to go?"

"What about your girlfriend?"

"And your husband?"

"He's fishing."

She uncrossed her arms and put her hands on her hips. Nothing was in her mouth but she swallowed anyway, shaking her head and saying mostly to herself, "This is crazy."

stratego

My mother kicked my father out when he sold her antique blueprint of our town's old baseball stadium. Her father was a city planner; he'd given it to her as a gift. But my father, patient only when bluffing a poker opponent, took the framed artifact off the wall, pawned it for fifty bucks, and returned home with a cartoonish, historical map of the town in the blueprint's frame.

One thing I'll say about my father, he was a persistent man, and still is today. In an attempt to calm my mother, he sat her down on our living room couch. Pacing, he launched into an undecipherable scheme about a poker game with a one-eyed man who spoke sign language, and his savant son who pretended to be deaf. This was his ship; he promised more change than a politician.

Mom let him finish, which involved an unrehearsed but theatrical performance of hand signals, head nods, and secret sideward glances between the three men; all played by my father. Then she stood up and walked over to her purse. She wrote a check, and emptied her wallet of cash.

"Take this," she said. "And don't you ever come back."

My father, stage left, glanced at me for a dramatic beat.

He approached my mother and held his hands a few inches from hers.

"If this is really what you want," he said. "Then I guess I'll do it."

She dropped the money on his feet.

"What was that like?" Merideth asks.

"It wasn't that bad. It's weird to watch your dad walk out the door, but we knew he'd be back. That was the bad part."

The coffeehouse is in the middle of town. I chose the location to see how much at risk we're willing to put ourselves. She must be a little worried about being seen. I certainly am, and she's got a lot more at stake. She really seems like she doesn't care though.

What I'm telling Merideth I've told maybe five people. "The worst was not letting him back in the house. He returned a few weeks later, when he knew mom would be at work. But she had already changed the locks."

"Good thinking," she says.

"I was home when he showed up. When I wouldn't open the door, he freaked."

Merideth looks great. She's wearing shorts, a little white T-shirt, and some oval-shaped tortoiseshell sunglasses. End of summer tan. She can't be any more than thirty-five.

"What did you do?" She asks.

"I didn't let him in. He was yelling and threatening me, but the choice was easy. The rule was: he wasn't allowed inside."

"Still—"

"Mom said the same thing. She felt terrible for me, but the situation was cut-and-dry. It just happened to involve my dad."

• • •

The flight home from Locust Valley last weekend was a nightmare. Half the passengers were infants. All of them cried. Even worse, faulty landing gear kept the plane on the runway for hours. Hope used this time to talk about our future. She knew she had me trapped.

"Will you be honest with me?" she asked.

"I'm always honest with you."

"Just tell me what you really think. Where do you see yourself in two years?"

"Hopefully off this plane."

"Seriously," she said.

"I don't know, Hope. What kind of a question is that?"

"I'm just curious. What are your goals? Where do you want to be, professionally and personally?"

"Well," I said, "job-wise, I'll probably be doing what I do now. But if I had my way, I'd work for myself."

"Doing what?"

"I haven't thought about it much because I'll never have the money, but it would be nice to have my own business."

"And what about your personal life?"

"Personally . . . couldn't tell ya."

The plane was supposed to take off at ten A.M.; it was noon. Everyone was cramped, the temperature was escalating. Boredom encouraged eavesdropping. Hope had been talking softly; my last answer silenced her completely. But it wasn't over. Living with a person gives you insight to his or her intimate patterns and habits. Hope is quietest right before she erupts.

"Jack, is it me, or is this relationship going nowhere?"

"Hope, we're sitting in the middle of a plane. This isn't exactly an ideal location for a heart-to-heart."

"You always have an excuse, don't you?"

"Since when do you like to talk about this stuff?"

"I just watched my two best friends get married, and I'm beginning to wonder about myself."

"You want to get married?"

"I'm not saying that, but eventually, yes. It would be nice to know if you feel the same way." She reached in the seat pocket in front of her and pulled out a deck of the airline's cards. We had already played every game we knew in the first hour of our delay. "I'll make you a deal," she said, shuffling. "One hand of blackjack. If I win, you see a therapist with me. If you win, I'll take you out to any restaurant you want."

"You mean like a couple's therapist?"

"I know of someone really good."

"Okay, but if I win, we don't have this conversation again until I say so."

I stuck with a hand of seventeen; she won with an ace and the queen of diamonds.

"So where are you right now?"

A little confused, she says, "I'm here."

"I know. But where did you say you'd be. Obviously not with me." A woman walks in carrying a baby in a backpack. The child is screaming. When the woman passes our table I say, "What if you knew her? What would you say?"

"I'd tell her you were a friend."

"Isn't that what I am?"

She laughs once and in an almost cold voice says, "I don't know what you are."

Yesterday a strange package arrived addressed to the sales department of our newspaper. No name was given. Three pictures accompanied a note written with letters cut out from magazines. One picture of a naked baby boy; another a picture of a graveyard cut from a recent article in our paper; and the final picture was a Polaroid taken from across the street from Sammy's. The people in the picture were too small to identify but my boss pointed to one and said, "That looks like you, Jack." The jagged letters in the note spelled out, "I can see your past. I can see your future. And I see you now."

When the plane finally took off the flight attendants began heating the prepared lunches. The smell of lasagna and marinated steak tips was pervasive. Hope picked up one of her fashion magazines immediately following her blackjack victory. The magazine's back cover was a car advertisement that said, "Redefining the American Dream." Beneath the quote a young woman stood next to a sporty, but relatively inexpensive convertible. Behind her was a well landscaped, pastel-colored apartment complex—no house, no picket fence, no children, no husband, no dogs.

When Hope tired of reading about how to have wavier hair, strong nails, and longer orgasms, she handed the magazine to me, noticed the ad, and laughed. "Advertisements. Who thinks buying a car will actually make their dreams come true?"

The woman in the ad was young, but strategically average looking. "Maybe owning that car is her dream," I said.

"Fine, but that's not the *American* Dream."

"The American Dream's a thing of the past. It's all about the individual now, America's too diverse for everyone to share the same goal. If you asked my dad, his version would involve a casino named after him and slot machines in every fast-food restaurant."

Hope smiled. "Diversity's a good thing. The ads are evil though. They promote the ridiculous idea that buying a car will make you happy."

"Depends. There are a lot of levels of happiness."

"Is that so?"

"I'll give you an example. The lasagne I just ate, I was happy with it. But I've been on this plane way too long and I was starving. If I went to a restaurant and shelled out twenty bucks and they brought me a little rectangle dish fresh from the microwave, I wouldn't be very happy."

"You're missing the point, Jack."

"No, I'm making the point, Hope."

After Mom's speech to me the night of her and Alice's interrogation, I decided Mom was right: I do need to decide if Hope is the one, and if she's not then I should get out. I've been making a real effort to be honest with myself about what it is I want out of a relationship and how that relationship will affect what I want out of life.

Hope looked at a man sitting across the aisle, and whispered, "What about him? What's his dream?"

The man wore large prescription glasses and had tangled hair jutting every direction off his scalp. He was about forty, and he made too much noise while trying to shoot down a spaceship on his laptop. He drank tomato juice, and picked peanuts one by one from a neatly organized pile on a napkin.

"One day," I said, "he hopes to meet a girl and lose his virginity."

We took turns making up other people's dreams, then Hope asked mine. I thought about the conversation we had on our first date about the young teenagers in love. I had worried about the boy's unshattered idealism. My response to Hope: "I hope that what I want out of life is the same as what I have."

Hope laced her fingers through my hand. She was silent for a minute, then whispered, "One day, I hope what I have is the same as what I want."

At the gate a wife and two daughters rushed the man with the laptop as Hope and I walked by in silence.

Before we left Long Island I actually got a chance to see my friends in Manhattan. None of them had girlfriends. We were riding the subway to Yankee Stadium, drinking Budweiser tallboys wrapped in brown paper bags. Bret stood, leaning against a pole for balance, and explained why there were no women in his life.

"There's too much temptation in this city. Everywhere you go your ego's being blitzed. Whether it's an ad on the side of a bus of some model in her underwear, or a jerk who bumps your shoulder walking down the street; whatever form, you're constantly being challenged. Images, people, attitudes are always coming at you."

"Sounds hectic," I said.

"Hectic? It's fun. What are you, *seventy?*"

Merideth grabs my elbow and whispers, "That's my neighbor."

"Is she friends with your husband?"

"No, she hates him. He got in a fight with her husband because their grass clippings kept blowing on our driveway every time he cut his lawn."

"What did he do?"

"He raked them into a pile and then dumped them on their doorstep."

"Nice temper." She doesn't laugh. "Why do you stay with him?"

"The answer to that would take forever."

If you build it, they will come. If you fake it, you better be convincing. Middle school plays have better props than the "therapist" Hope has selected. In an effort to be convincing, "Dr. Reeny" has stacked pamphlets she lifted from somewhere, offering solutions for same-sex couples, newly-weds, couples impaired because of substance abuse, and relationships hindered because of a newborn. There's no category for Hope and me, and nowhere under the heading "Choosing the Right Therapist" does it say "Play charades instead."

I should leave but the doctor's a knockout: wavy black hair, hazel eyes, and a face straight out of a New England clothing catalogue. She dresses just like Hope: very fashionable and perfect for her body type. Her shirt is blue silk, short-sleeved, and button down, and her black skirt so mini, her underwear flashes every time she crosses her legs. Sitting three feet away from me, her arms hang at her side in an attempt to have body language as open as possible, making her breasts stick out. They're absolutely perfect and I wonder if she used the same plastic surgeon as Hope. Maybe I should ask her if that is where they met.

"What are you thinking?" She asks, uncrossing her legs, then crossing them the other way.

Her underwear looks violet. "Not to be rude, but how old are you?"

"We're really here to talk about you, Jack." Hope will be here in half an hour, then she'll meet with "Dr. Reeny" alone. Afterwards, the three of us will "talk" together.

"You know, my girlfriend set this up, so I'm not really sure what I'm supposed to say."

She looks at a yellow pad of paper on her desk. "I have some notes; if you like, I can lead the conversation."

"This should be interesting."

"I understand a friend of yours died not too long ago. Often in these circumstances the result can be reckless behavior, seclusion, intense pessimism or unjustified anger. Do any of these remind you of yourself?"

"I'm not here to talk about Mark."

"You're here to talk about yourself."

"I'm here because I lost a game of fucking blackjack. You can ask me anything you want about Hope, but when I want to talk about Mark, I'll make the appointment myself."

"I understand."

"Sorry," I say.

"I shouldn't have been so careless. Why don't you tell me about Hope." She recrosses her legs again, slowly, and pretty soon I'm telling Hope stories I never even thought about. Knowing that Dr. Reeny is a phony, and that everything I say will be told directly to Hope, I figure it's an easy way to earn some brownie points. She listens to me for a long time, then says, "When are you most happy with her?"

Without having to think, I describe a Friday night ritual. After work Hope and I meet at home and walk to the grocery store. Slowly we make our way down the aisles, picking out items for only that night. On our way home we see people beginning their evening. We smile and say hello, knowing our evening's entertainment is being carried in a brown paper bag. That's what I like the most—that feeling of companionship.

Single, Friday nights were like a sport, always pressure,

with time running out. But now, with Hope, we've got our own venue, our own rules, without a ticking clock.

"That's all we have time for," Dr. Reeny says.

When she opens her office door Hope walks in, hugs her, and says, "Sarah, it's so good to see you again. You look amazing."

"You know each other?" I say, playing dumb.

"Sarah was my big sister in our sorority." Hope smiles at her affectionately, as Dr. Reeny tells me to wait outside.

When I'm summoned back to the "office," Dr. Reeny says she's encouraged and suggests we find a common goal to work toward as a couple. She reminds Hope to call her about dinner next week and walks us to the door.

Afterwards, Hope offers to buy dinner and picks my favorite restaurant. When we finish, she suggests we walk around and go shopping.

Hope's at the counter signing a credit card slip. She writes her name quickly, shutting the bag before I get close. "What did you get?"

"Here, it's for you." Inside the bag, wrapped in beige tissue, is a dress shirt I pointed out when we walked into the store.

"What did you do that for?" I ask.

"You said you liked it."

"I do like it, but that doesn't mean I want you to buy it for me."

"Just take it and let me do something nice."

At the next store she buys a tie when I'm not looking. I tell her if she feels guilty for sending me to a phony shrink, buying me stuff isn't the solution.

"I'm desperate Jack. All I hear from my mom is how you

and I are wrong for each other and all I want to do is make things work between us. When I asked you on the plane where you wanted to be in the future you said, *"Off this plane, I hope."* That doesn't help me. I need real answers and I can't wait much longer."

"But Hope, a fake therapist?"

"Jack, I'm living two lives." She puts the clothes in the bag. "I don't want to give up my life with you, and it isn't possible to give up my life back home."

"Why not?"

Hope pulls me into an ice-cream shop. Tinted windows, a propped-open door, and the day's leftover air-conditioning make things cool and inviting. The air, flushed with the scent of vanilla, makes me want to sit and simply breathe. On the menu are pictures of fudge-covered sundaes, fruit smoothies, and frozen chocolate bars on sticks. After much deliberation we decide to split what's called an American Cream shake, a root beer float with a fancy name.

"Jack, there's something you don't know." Hope takes a sip from the shake and looks down at her bracelets. "I don't quite know how to say this. But, when my dad died, he left me a lot of money." She looks like she confessed a crime.

"I can't tell you how many times my mother said never to tell anyone about my inheritance. She made it seem like the money was more important than me."

The tint in the windows slowly lightens, as the sky outside gets dark. For the first time Hope is eager to talk about her past, and counts off story after story with the zeal of a child returning home from summer camp. She tells me about beach houses with narrow hallways and small rooms facing the Atlantic. Cucumber sandwiches, nannies with Caribbean accents, clay tennis courts, and ponies named April and

May all surface. And though she's talking to me, her mind is in a different time and place, remembering, releasing. She talks the entire walk home and falls asleep on the couch listening to music.

Besides pepperoni, what rhymes with bologna? Sammy called me in this Friday because he's going out of town and isn't sure he'll be back by Tuesday to place his ad.

Sammy says, "How 'bout coney? Enjoy some bologna then have an ice cream coney? What do you think?"

"I think you missed your calling on Madison Avenue."

"And I think you haven't come up with anything much better."

Sammy's got a surplus of bologna. I didn't ask, but he said the distributor messed up his order. He wants to offer a two-for-one special on any bologna sandwich.

"I think my girlfriend wants to get married."

"You're too young, now give me a word."

"I'm serious."

"I'm not? Don't be an idiot. You got time, I don't. I gotta catch a plane."

"How about, Don't be a phony, admit you love bologna. Maybe we'll pull a few meat eaters out of the vegetarian closet."

"I like it. You know that guy's written something on my window every day this week."

I lean forward. "Like what?" If you catch the guy, are you going to kill him? Let's do a stakeout one night, what do you say, you and me, a baseball bat, a couple of guns, and I know you got a switchblade on you somewhere. Let's do it.

"I don't pay attention. It's just some stupid kid. I'm just getting tired of having to clean up every morning."

"I'll come by while you're gone, keep things clean."

"Yeah?" Sammy stands and puts on the jacket of his shiny, olive green suit. "You'd do that for me?"

"Sammy?" I stick my arms out and look confused, "Forgeddabouddit."

"That's why I love and worry about you. You're a little off, but it's good. If you have a ring on your finger when I get back though, I'm gonna chop it off and tape it to your forehead."

Half a block from Sammy's Merideth is hunched over on a bench. When she sees me she keeps her head down.

"Merideth? Are you all right?"

Her eyes are red. "Yeah. I mean, no."

"What happened?" Obviously Merideth's marriage is doomed but I still thought she had a good grasp on things. Finding her crying in public is as shocking as it is upsetting.

"Nothing you can change. You want to get a drink?" We're right in the middle of town, which is too risky to try again, so we get in her car and drive to an out-of-the-way café, converted from an old gasoline station.

Merideth is dressed in tight navy blue pants and a black blazer over a red silk shirt. Her hair is styled and she's wearing lipstick. I've never seen her out of sneakers. Her four-wheel drive has a sunroof and disc player. The toughest terrain it battles is the speed bumps in her son's kindergarten parking lot, but SUVs are popular with wealthy moms—the anti–status symbol status symbol.

We sit in the corner with our drinks. Merideth talks first, "I've never done this before, and I guess I just want to know, why me?"

I'm looking at this woman. If I didn't know better I'd

think she has it all. She's beautiful, wears nice clothes, and drives a fancy car. She's been married to the same man for many years; they have two children. I'm sure other women see their family somewhere—in a restaurant or on a vacation—and sigh, telling themselves life isn't fair. She tells me she's unsure how to act, or what to say. I want to tell her to shut up—that she's giving me too much information, and if I had my choice, I'd rather not know better.

I rush home because it's Friday night, and for the first time in months, Hope and I are going out. Her boss is having a barbecue.

Hope sits on a hand-painted kitchen stool, husking an ear of corn. Still dressed up from work, her shirt hangs untucked from her skirt. Her hair has been let down as well, and covers part of her face. "You're sick," she says.

"What do you mean?"

"That's our excuse. Let's stay home for dinner. Where have you been?"

"Am I late?"

"A little."

"I guess I took my time."

Hope fills a pot with water and puts it on the stove to boil. "I thought we'd eat, then walk over to the video store and rent a movie. You want a beer?"

"Please," I say.

Hope unscrews the cap as she hands the bottle to me, smiling a first real hello. "Did you have a good day?"

Hope had been looking forward to her boss's barbecue for a long time. Dr. Reeny must have broken our mock patient–mock doctor confidentiality. Hope is all smiles now, plucking strands of almost invisible hair from between the rows of corn. Tonight she'll be on her best behavior; tomorrow she'll bring up marriage. She started in with the wedding magazines before we left for Long Island. I should have sensed the pressure mounting. Too many pictures of tiered cakes, happy couples, ideal churches, and personal ceremonies for a girl to take. But Merideth sits on a bench, crying in the center of town, with her back bent forward and the butts of her hands pressed hard into her eye sockets—a perfect cover shot for a magazine about divorce. But then, who would ever subscribe?

I can see your past. I can see your future. And I see you now. Your world is coming to an end.

"My day?" I say, "I'm just glad it's over."

twister

I didn't respond to Dad's letter asking for an "amicable relationship." He hasn't written me again yet, but someone sent
me an anonymous envelope containing only a pack of
matches. Written inside the cover was, "Don't play with fire."
The matches are from a deli here in town called Tiny Tim's
Super Heroes. It used to be Dad's favorite place to take me for
lunch. All the sandwiches were named after superheroes;
Dad used to get the Batmoburger.

I went to the deli to see if the current matchbooks had a different design, but Tiny Tim's had gone out of business; a pipe
shop selling incense and bongs took its place. A cashier emit-
ting a faint smell of marijuana wore an old T-shirt that said,
"Your world is coming to an end. Recycle Now." I showed him
the matches, asking if they could be ten years old. He nodded
his head slowly and said, "Look pretty new to me, dude."

We're sitting in the front of Merideth's car, parked in the lot
of a small playground close to her house. The Continental is
to our right. Hope went out with Dr. Reeny and a few
friends. Merideth's husband is fishing again.

I ask her, "Does he ever forget to take his fishing pole?"
She replies, "Sometimes," in a confessional tone.

"Why do you stay?"

"My kids."

"Shouldn't of had them."

"Actually, I thought they'd save us."

"That was a gamble."

"Yeah, but they're the best thing in my life, so either way I guess I won. Why do you stay?" After hearing about Hope's past concerning her father, and then about how her mother behaves, Merideth said I was getting involved in an unhealthy situation. She said I was, and will be, nothing more than a foot soldier in Hope's war against her mother for independence and forgiveness.

"Hope's a good person. She had a tough time growing up and her mom still hasn't forgiven her. If anything, I think she deserves a little credit for how well she handles herself."

Reclining her seat all the way back she says, "Are you more afraid of being alone, or making a commitment?"

"My dad scares me. He's a desperate man. I'm pretty sure he killed his sister because he wanted to sell her car. Insanity is in his bloodstream and I once locked him out of his own house. I'm much easier a target if I'm alone." But of course I don't say this. Instead: "Hey, I do love her, and I don't want to lose her. Hope's got a lot to offer. I just wish I had more time."

After Dr. Reeny had brought up Mark, I found myself thinking about how shaky the future is. The thought of marrying Hope became very appealing; a risk perhaps, getting married too soon, but a marriage would put me on the path toward a "regular life." I thought of all the stumbling blocks in my little self-improvement plan and quite frankly there's just way too many.

"Well if you don't want to lose her, maybe you should give it a try. Just wait a while before you have kids."

Taking a moment to consider this, I move my own seat back so we're parallel. "And they wonder why half of all marriages fail."

"I hate to break it to you, Jack, but marriage isn't only about love and happiness. A lot of the times it dissolves to nothing but a business agreement. If you manage to stay friends, you should consider yourself lucky."

Alice, the founder of the Drinking Club, removed herself from the group for the six months her second marriage lasted. The Friday before her wedding, Mom threw her a Leaving the Club party. Alice had just returned from a trip she'd taken to Mexico with a few of her married friends. While visiting the country, almost all the women had enjoyed dalliances to differing extents.

From the kitchen I heard Alice defend her actions, staunchly stating, "Hey, I was about to get married. Why not have one last shot at a good time?"

Alice's fiancé may not have agreed, but after listening to both Merideth and the Drinking Club, a difference in standards for the rules governing relationships between the Young and Old could not have been more blatant. To say who's right and who's wrong could be an endless debate, but clearly, one group is more realistic, or maybe the other is trying to live up to an ideal.

Trying to live up to an ideal is exactly what I think about when I think about Breach. We shared some strong emotions and had the support of everyone around us. She's been seeing someone for a while now and it sounds like they're pretty serious. He's a good guy, a little older than me, successful, and, according to Alice, *"Very handsome."* I have to admit I was a little jealous to hear that, but Breach summed it up best in a short email she'd sent me a few weeks ago:

Heard you had a good time in Low-Cost Valley, Hope should be wanting that rock anytime now. You'll always have my best wishes because I know I'll always have yours, but then again Jack, I wouldn't want to put any pressure on you. Stop by and meet the beau sometime but leave the wine at home . . . you missed Last Call. Love always, Breach.

Merideth shut her eyes and sighed a deep breath. "I wish I could be more supportive, Jack."

Shutting my eyes too, I reached over and grabbed Merideth's wrist lightly. She flinched, but then let me hold her hand.

hope's rules

Hope wrote this note in a card that came with an engagement present. She bought me a watch. It's big, has a stainless steel linked wristband, and is water-resistant up to two hundred meters.

Jack,

You need to know that I love you for who you are. I'm so happy to be marrying someone different than the men I grew up with. All my life I've wanted to break away, and then you came along and made it possible.

But please understand, take this as a warning, there will be hurdles for us to jump. The people back home will see you as an outsider, and will treat you that way. But they are shallow, close minded, sheltered, and all the other things I resist. Together we can overcome them.

My mother will not be happy. She had different plans for me. But she will also be the one dealing with these people on a daily basis. I have to think of her. So what I am trying to say is this, if you hear me tell a little white lie about us, or you, don't be shocked, and please, don't think I am ashamed of you. I'm not. I love you. I'm just trying to protect my mother. I owe her at least that, and so much more.

Love,
Hope

I read the note, and the watch was awesome, but I had to say something. "Pardon me, but it's not like I'm some kind of heathen. I went to college. I work for a living. So maybe I'm a Democrat, but I still maintain I'm a better citizen than Sonny, Bunny, and Alden put together."

"You're missing the point, Jack. I totally agree. If I didn't I wouldn't be marrying you. But you don't understand these people."

We were sitting in the kitchen drinking coffee. It was early in the morning. Neither of us had gotten dressed for work.

"Why do you care what they think?"

"I don't. But they're gonna talk and it's all going to end up in my mother's face. I just want to try and save her some grief, which in turn, will save me some grief."

I looked at the watch. It was set to the correct time, and ticking. "Fine. Say what you have to, but I'm not taking golf lessons."

Hope laughed and slid the watch over my wrist. It was too big but she said we'd get the band adjusted later.

candyland

"When they said Jack was in jail, I couldn't believe it. How many men get arrested on their honeymoon?" Hope is telling this now-famous story to a large table at her mother's Christmas party. A formal affair, men are wearing coats and ties, women have slinked into dresses bought only for the five hours this party will last. We got back from Maui two days ago and came straight to Locust Valley. This is probably the tenth time Hope has told the story, and she hasn't gotten tired of it yet.

It is fantastic. The plot's got everything: movie stars, the beach, a car chase, and the Hawaiian police. Hope tells it best. She's great at holding an audience captive and tonight she'll have quite a crowd. Hope's mother is well known for her annual Christmas party. There's going to be as many people here as there were at our wedding. The same people for the most part. I met them all at Bunny and Grayson's wedding, then again at Alden and Tianna's. It's one big traveling social circuit, a really fancy circus, with no three rings, only sideshows.

My mother was upset she wouldn't see me over Christmas; this is the first time we've spent the holiday apart. Hope and I bought her a really great present though. We found the old blueprint of the baseball stadium my dad had hocked, and bought it back. Mom was speechless but suddenly looked worried while she stared at the gift. Angling the print in my direction she said, "You better be careful. He's gonna find you." I didn't tell her he already had.

Mom wasn't pleased about the marriage in the first place. She didn't agree with my argument that Hope's wealth would ease many of the pressures that most young couples face.

"And that's why your marriage will work," she said, "because Hope is rich?" She shook her head. "You have so much to learn it's frightening." I was about to speak but she held up her hand. "But you know what? Fine. Get married, learn the hard way, and I'll see you back here sooner than you think."

"Jesus, Mom."

"Honey, I just want what's best for you. This isn't it."

"Well, I hope you'll at least come to the wedding."

"You don't want to listen, do you? You actually think I'm gonna travel to watch this happen?"

"Great. So I'll have no parents there."

Mom pinched the bridge of her nose and shut her eyes as tight as she could. After a moment she sighed. "I'll go, Jack, not because I support your decision, but because if I don't, you might do something stupid like try and track down your dad."

Mom feels guilty for not providing a father figure. We talked about it once. I told her she did the right thing, throwing Dad out, and that I was proud of her decision. It was my eighteenth birthday; we were at a Chinese restaurant. She said every boy should have a man around, and I promised I hadn't missed a thing. An extra fortune cookie came with the bill and I couldn't help but think it was a sign from some higher being. Or maybe it was just Dad, secretly watching us from behind a newspaper, wearing a cheap wig and a fake mustache, hunched in a booth at the back of the restaurant.

If Mom knew about Dad's strange antics, her worries would be diverted from the marriage. But I can't tell her. I tell myself I'm protecting her.

As predicted, Hope's mother wasn't happy either. I listened on the other phone while Hope broke the news—Hope said it was the best way for me to understand what she was up against. I'd been giving her a hard time about having to lie about me. After listening to her mother, I haven't said a word about it. But while listening I had to speak up. Her mother said this: "Jack is nothing but a phase in your life. You're rebelling but in a year or two you'll see your mistake and it will cost you a lot of money to fix it."

I said, "Listen, write up any kind of prenuptial agreement you want, and I'll sign it. If it doesn't work between us I promise to walk away quietly. Just give your daughter your blessing."

Silence from the other line. Hope filled it: "Fine, Mom, you know what? Jack and I will just elope to Las Vegas. We'll have a nice five-minute ceremony at a drive-in chapel and I'll make sure to take pictures and send them to all your friends back home. You think you can control me? Stop us."

We won. The thought of Hope not being married at GreadeRock, as well as her mother not being able to plan everything, was too frightening. I still haven't signed a prenup.

Thirteen husbands, eleven trophy wives, two originals, one widow, one widower, and a stag that is Hornblower have arrived. The first thing they want is a drink, the second, to hear the honeymoon story.

Hope sits at a round, white plastic table set by the catering company this afternoon. Her dress is black, barely supported by spaghetti straps, and cinched in at the waist, stopping just short of her knees. She loves having an audience and gets better with every narration, finding her pace, skipping a detail here, adding a few of her own there—calculated changes to smooth the tale, keep the listeners happy.

I had gotten arrested for disturbing the peace, and was also charged with speeding and reckless driving. I pleaded guilty and was fined.

Because so many people have gathered, Hope sits on the table, so everyone can see her. "It was our first day," she begins, "so we drove to a beach, about a mile away. We'd heard James Kidder was staying at our hotel with Joy Fleecer. We hadn't seen them until that morning, when they walked past us on the beach."

Because of their good looks, high asking prices, and strong Box Office returns, James Kidder and Joy Fleecer have been dubbed "Hollywood's Power Couple of the New Millennium" by several entertainment magazines. Our brush with fame sends murmurs through the crowd. A couple of the females inquire about James Kidder, asking if he looks as good in real life as he does in the movies. Hope pretends to wipe sweat off her forehead, then shaking her hand says, "I tell you, I had only been married one day, but I was ready to run off with him at the drop of a hat." Hope winks and smiles at me while everyone laughs at her joke.

"I wasn't sure it was them. They were wearing sunglasses and baseball hats. I don't know why, but I had to find out. I asked Jack to follow with me, but he told me I should leave them alone. He was probably right, but I got up and started walking anyway."

The doorbell rings. I volunteer to answer, trying to be helpful, and keep things friendly between me and Hope's mother. Alden and Tianna are at the door along with Alden's father and the party's twelfth trophy wife. Normally Tianna wouldn't ring before coming inside but it's a party and she needs to make an entrance in her new dress. Alden looks like a life-sized Christmas ornament. His blazer is bright red, pants green, and the tie is patterned red and white with candy cane stripes. A fake, white beard covers the bottom of his face, and slung over his shoulder is a red velvet sack, from which he hands me a chocolate Santa. Tianna's dress is dark green and cut exactly like Hope's. Her shoes are green and curled at the toe, like an elf's. Hope's got the spotlight though, so their entrance goes unnoticed.

Alden says, "Let's talk business," and pulls me to the bar. The more I know Alden, the less I like him. "Quit your job, Jack." He's got a gleam in his eye as he takes a sip of his cocktail. "It's time for you and I to go into business for ourselves. Make some real money. What do you say?" His drink drips through his phony beard. He'd forgotten it was on his face.

Alden's a slippery guy. His affable nature is deceiving in that he's so outgoing his manipulative juggling is often overshadowed. I've caught him lying a few times but never mentioned it, not wanting to stir the waters. "What's your plan, Santa?"

"Let's make our own beer and sell it. A microbrew company."

"And how are we going to do that? Enlist a core of elves?"

"I talked to Tianna, she talked to Hope, they're both

excited and think it's a great idea. I know a guy who makes fruit-flavored beer. He's interested. If we can draw up a solid business plan, we're golden." He takes his beard off after dribbling his drink a second time.

"What the hell is fruit-flavored beer?"

"It's beer with a fruity taste. Girls will love it, and people who normally don't drink beer will have an alternative. It's like we're creating a whole new market."

"I don't know a thing about the beer business."

"Neither do I, but we'll learn. The important thing is we have the idea and we got the money."

"The money comes from Hope and Tianna?"

"Yup."

"And they're comfortable with this? How come Hope never mentioned it?"

"She loves the idea. You think she wants to be married to a guy selling ad space for the rest of her life?"

"Yeah, but Alden, we don't even live in the same state. How are we gonna be business partners?"

"Don't worry about the details, Jack. It's Christmastime. Let's celebrate." He bends over to pick up his bag of goodies.

"Is Adrian coming tonight?"

"Good question." He slings the sack over his shoulder. "I don't think he's coming out this year."

Alden walks in the direction of Hope's performance. She's gotten to the part where I go to our rental car to get my flip-flops. She tells it with me going to get a book. She doesn't mind my flip-flops, but the closest thing to a flip-flop at GreadeRock is when a kid lands on his back in the water after trying to do a somersault off the high dive.

I had gone to get the sandals to try and catch up with

Hope. My feet were blistered from dancing in the tight shoes at the wedding reception, so walking long distances barefoot was out of the question. The trouble started in the parking lot, on my way back from the car.

From behind someone taps my shoulder. Hope's mother hands me a cordless phone.

The person at the end of the line shouts, "Jack! Happy holidays, son!"

Immediately I duck into a den designed for intimate conversation. Small in size, the room has thick, glass French doors to keep noise out. Bookshelves built into the wall are surrounded by dark-stained wood, a red carpet covers most of the floor. A leather armchair that looks never sat in and a red couch with fluffed cushions are the only furniture. I sit on a leather statue of a hippopotamus meant to be used as a footrest. There's also a gaudy, foot-high figurine of a Santa Claus that makes an appearance once a year, only because it was a gift from someone close to the family who still comes to the party.

"Dad?" I say, "What are you doing?"

"Can't a father wish his son a Merry Christmas?"

"Sure, but it's better if you do it every year, not once a decade. How'd you get this number?"

"It was on your answering machine. What's all this about you being married, you devil?"

"You didn't get the invitation?"

"Don't kid a kidder, Jack." He's calling from a pay phone in the lobby of a casino. The high-pitched music of chiming bells plays in the background.

"Where are you?"

"Actually Jack, that's why I'm calling. I'm right down the

street. I thought I'd stop by and say hello. Meet me at the back door in ten minutes."

"Dad, you can't come over here. You don't even know these people."

"Well I see things haven't changed much. Still keeping your old man out of the house, eh boy?"

"Dad, what do you want from me?" He doesn't answer so I continue. "Do you want to be friends or do you want to send me matches that say don't play with fire? What is that anyway? A threat?"

"I didn't send you any matches. I do want to be friends, though."

"Look, Dad, I gotta go. Write me again. I promise to write you back this time."

"Hey wait a minute, I said I was coming over. Now meet me out back."

"Are you trying to scare me?"

"Where do you get these ideas? I just want to say hello."

"Dad, I know you're not in Locust Valley. I can hear the casino in the background."

Before Dad hangs up he says, "I just want to make things up to you."

I walk back into the party. Midstory, Hope sets her drink down and checks her dress, to make sure she's not revealing any parts of her that should not be revealed. "A group of Hawaiian kids in a pickup truck almost runs him over, and one of them gives him the finger." Hope gives the crowd the finger, winning a riotous response. "So Jack does it back," she shows her finger again, getting an even bigger laugh than the first one, "and they circle the truck around and drive by him once more, this time close enough for a girl to pluck his visor right off the top of his head." This hushes the crowd; none of them can bear to look my direction. "Then they drove off, yelling and laughing at Jack."

I had been wearing a cowboy hat, not a visor. It was old, bent, made from straw with a worn, sweat-stained black band. I'd owned it for years. The hat wasn't an obnoxious, ten-gallon, Texan affair, but something a farmer might wear. Simple, yet effective, the sun never burned my neck or face. That first morning in our hotel room Hope had said, "I can't believe I'm married to someone who wears a cowboy hat to the beach."

I shrugged my shoulders, smiled, and said, "For better or worse, baby."

Hope took a long look at me and said, "Actually, you look adorable, but this is a fancy hotel and they kind of expect their guests to dress appropriately."

"Oh, and a Japanese man wearing a banana hammock *is* appropriate?"

She laughed. "I know, but a sweaty old farmer's hat isn't either."

In the lobby she bought me a visor with the hotel's logo on it.

"I'm not wearing this," I said, and handed it back to her.

"Hey, I just bought it."

"I'm not a visor kind of guy, Hope. I don't own tennis whites, and I've never worn wristbands or boating shoes. Sorry."

"What the hell does that mean?"

The lobby was an enormous marble tunnel, a palm tree–lined entrance at one end, and a long deck facing the ocean at the opposite side. Everything appeared larger than normal—the pillars, the flowerpots, even the sound of our voices. Doormen were dressed in Hawaiian shirts and white pants; hostesses wore muumuus and leis. Tourists left in khakis and blazers, while others arrived in ungodly patterned island wear.

"Fine," I said. "Give me the visor."

We sat, two angry newlyweds, trying to outlast each other's silence, with the Pacific Ocean at our feet and the sun shining behind us.

I lost.

"Sorry Hope, but I can feel my neck burning. I'm gonna get my hat."

"Why don't you just turn around?"

"Because I'd rather face the ocean than the parking lot."

"But you look really good in that visor."

"And if I wear it any longer the sun's gonna burn a hole through my neck."

"Do whatever you want, Jack. I'm gonna go for a walk. I'll see you when I get back."

Hope had never invited me to join her, nor was she following any movie stars. She crossed the actors on her way back. She tells the story differently because no one wants to hear about a couple fighting on their honeymoon. I felt bad the second she left and went to the car to get my flip-flops so I could run after her. While getting the flops, the hat was only on my head for a minute; I had been planning on leaving it in the car in an attempt to appease Hope.

"This is the part of the story I have trouble believing," Hope says. "Jack got in the car and started chasing the truck." She pauses, but the house is unsure how to react. "When he catches up he starts honking and once the kids realize who's following them, they start passing the visor around, taking turns trying it on and pretending to throw it off the side of the road. A policeman driving the other direction makes a U-turn and pulls Jack over."

I remember being surprised by my own reaction, but I'd had the hat forever and like a good pair of jeans, the sentimental value was more important than the object.

Sammy had said this concerning my marriage: "If you're happy, Jack. I'm happy." Then he chuckled. "Young people," he said, "always rushing until something finally slows 'em down."

"I'm happy," I said. "And you said it yourself, right? 'You only live once.'"

"Jack, I'm flattered, but don't go living by my words. Really."

"Don't worry, Sammy, you didn't exactly coin the phrase."

He laughed, shook my hand and congratulated me. Then he handed me an envelope with my full name written on the outside. Someone had slipped it beneath the door earlier that week. Inside was a card congratulating both Hope and me. Our engagement announcement from the newspaper had been cut out and stapled to the inside of the card. My eyes had been blacked out and tears were drawn pouring down Hope's face. The message said, "Don't blink boy, you've got a wife to think about." The card was signed with a question mark.

Hope's mother needs me in the kitchen. The catering staff works around us while we sit at a breakfast table. Hope's mother seems hurried and somewhat out of character: a little too drunk, probably from the stress of the event. Inside a folder are papers decorated with red adhesive, arrow-shaped labels that say, SIGN YOUR NAME HERE, pointing at a blank line, dated December fourth. Our wedding was on the fifth, almost twenty days ago.

Hope's mother hands me a pen and leaves the table, distracted by a wheel of Brie that's been sliced asymmetrically. Spinning quickly toward me she almost trips saying, "Now where'd I put that pen?"

"You just gave it to me."

"Oh, and our lawyer, you'll meet him; he's here tonight." She turns to a caterer, "Not there!" She takes a few steps toward a sink full of dishes, but hastily turns around.

"Should Hope be here for this?"

"No. If you have any questions I can get our lawyer, but I promise it's very fair."

"I'm sure it is," I say. "Besides, we'll never see these again, right?"

She clinks my drink with her own and says, "That's the spirit." Then she turns to the remaining wait staff and says, "Why don't you all go out and see if anyone needs a drink." They leave as she spins again toward the sink, turning on the water.

My boss at the paper cherishes my attention to detail. In the two years I've worked there, I've yet to lose us money with a silly mistake. For this reason, many of my clients are the bar owners who prefer to do business over drinks. Some salesmen have horror stories of alcohol-impaired contract signings. So far my record's clean.

Hope's mother accidentally splashes water across the front of her shirt. "Oh dear God!"

"Here, let me get those." I quickly sign my name, adding a small number two, correcting the date, December fourth, to tonight's date, the twenty-fourth. I close the folders and grab a towel. Her dress is so wet it clings to her belly button.

"It's not that bad," I say, stooped over, dabbing the towel at her stomach.

She raises her arms so I can get at her midsection better, then she rests them over my shoulders. One hand wedges under my shirt collar while the other begins to rub the back of my head. Her voice loses its edge and becomes almost confessional. "How embarrassing, I've always been so careless." The hand at my head reaches down and pulls up her shirt so she can check the water stain. Her breasts are exposed—no bra. "Jack," she says, "did you know Hope and I have the same breasts?"

This is true. Two years ago they went to the same doctor and got matching enhancements. Hope said she only agreed to it because she figured her mother was having a midlife crisis and wanted to help any way she could. It's a rather bizarre family secret, but Hope looks fantastic in a bathing suit, which is why I wasn't that surprised James Kidder took the time to talk to her.

I'm frozen, still stooped over, trying to figure out not only Hope's mother's motivation for flashing me, but also how I can get out of the situation.

"Jack, tell me if you can feel a difference. I'm aging and I need to know. It's OK, really." Her voice is soft and drunk, "I'm a very lonely woman, Jack."

"Ms. Witherspoon, maybe you've had a little too much to drink, or maybe it's the holidays, but one thing I know for a fact is that you're gonna have to try a lot harder than that to sabotage my marriage."

Suddenly sounding very sober she says, "Jack, honey, I'm just getting started."

I follow her out of the kitchen. As we approach Hope's table her mother lifts the folder. Hope nods at her and says,

"We need you for this part, Jack." Apparently everyone wants to hear me tell the segment about how and why I got arrested. Hope pats a space on the table next to her.

"The whole situation is rotten," I say. "I just wanted my hat back."

Tianna winks. She knows the real story. Hope tells her everything; she even called her on the first night of our honeymoon. Hope had begun to cry as the limo drove us from the wedding reception. I put an arm around her and said, "I know you're scared, Hope, but you didn't make the wrong decision. Your family and friends aren't going anywhere."

She grabbed my hand and said, "No matter what happens, I love you, Jack." She called Tianna from our suite and everything was settled. Tianna, Hope explained, was her only friend on our side.

Hornblower pipes up, "Why so attached to a visor, Jack?"

I ignore him. "The cop pulls me over and says, 'Do you know why I stopped you?' And I say, 'It doesn't take a genius.' And he goes, 'What's that supposed to mean?' And I say, 'Well, it was me or the locals, right?' Then he tells me to get out of the car and says he doesn't like my attitude. Now I'm really mad, so I slam the car door and he arrests me for disturbing the peace."

Hope takes over and tells about getting me released from custody, leaving out the part about how I was also being held for car theft because her name was on the rental agreement, since she was paying.

Afterwards we talk in a corner. "Who called you?"

"My dad. He's coming over. He should be here in half an hour."

"What?"

"Just kidding. He called to say Merry Christmas, that's all."

She steps closer, pressing her hand into mine. "Are you all right?"

"I'm fine. This time of year is tough for some people. He's probably lonely."

Hope motions toward the party and says, "No kidding. Mom started doing this the year after Dad died. She's still a wreck. I think she's already had one too many spritzers tonight."

"I helped her out in the kitchen. She made quite a little mess."

To me, the people only look familiar; I don't know the private details of their lives. But I'm almost certain that everyone has a reason to be melancholy. Holidays are deceiving: meant to bring joy, but universal participation, combined with a specific annual date, always reminds us of those lost, hurt, or excluded. This is when we pull our own legs, masquerading in Christmas cheer and Yuletide spirit. Emotional hocus-pocus to make the long lost relatives, betrayed friends, and bad marriages disappear until normal life can return with the new year's calendar and the routine of the everyday. I always make sure to send Mark's family a card with a long letter about what's going on in my life. His mother called me the year I broke up with Breach and said, "Jack, what happened?"

"Your mom gave me the papers to sign."

Hope looks at the toe of her shoe. "Thanks for dealing with that. I hope it helps."

"No big deal," I say. "Just so long as you'll buy me a new hat."

She smiles and says, "That can be arranged." Laughing, she steps back and raises both our arms like we've just finished a waltz. She checks me from head to toe, admiring the suit she gave me as an early Christmas present. "Look at you, all dressed up. I swear," she says, shaking her head.

Merideth was half an hour late for our walk the day I told her my plans to marry Hope, and that we'd have to stop seeing each other.

"Sorry I'm so late," she said. "My son's teacher called me because he decked some kid."

"He's only in first grade."

She shrugged, "I know, but you want to hear the cutest thing? He was telling me about this girl he likes and how they were going to get married."

When I told her about the marriage, she didn't seem upset, or even all that disappointed. But her expression resembled a humored type of sympathy; probably not altogether different than my own expression the day Hope and I first had lunch on the deck at Willie Ryan's as I watched the young boy in first-love slurp his milk shake, completely unaware of the storm awaiting him, not being warned by me because, really, there's just no other way to learn than on your own.

Tianna and Alden join Hope and me in the corner. Hornblower approaches with a camera.

"Mr. Hornblower," Hope says, "did you volunteer to be the photographer again this year?"

"You betcha, kiddo. Now the four of you squeeze together, and on the count of three, say cheese."

trivial pursuit

I didn't make a New Year's resolution. This upset Hope so I promised to stop eating french fries for a year.

"That's the dumbest thing I've ever heard," she said. "What's the point?"

"It's sort of healthy. And since when do you need a point?"

"The purpose of a resolution is self-improvement. You pick a goal and stay committed."

"I'm not gonna quit my job for Alden's harebrained scheme."

"Jack, he *knows* people. You guys will have a lot of help. You said you wanted to have your own business; this is your chance."

"Listen, if it makes you happy, I'll do it. But I'm telling you now, Alden's clueless and I'm gonna lose my job. Then what?"

"I promise, Jack, we're not going to starve."

"You're standing there telling me you'd rather be married to a guy with no job than one with a job that your mother doesn't admire?"

"I know Jack, we're all crazy."

(I never told Hope about her mother's antics in the

kitchen. Two reasons: 1. I don't want to upset Hope. 2. That's exactly what her mother wants me to do.)

"But Hope," I say, "I thought you wanted to get *away* from Locust Valley?"

"You're looking at this the wrong way. This is a great opportunity for you. Be optimistic."

Alden had created quite a buzz with his microbrew plan. He inspired us all with talk of reaching a niche market, making millions, and fulfilling our destiny. We stayed in Locust Valley the entire month of January. My original marriage and honeymoon vacation plans allowed for three weeks off, but Hope and Alden extended my leave. I met with Alden and several others about the building of our fruit-powered empire. Hope did stuff with her mother. In the end it was a bust. Alden's connections were hard-pressed to find a way to profit from his idea. People seemed to think beer mixed with fruit was unappealing. The taste test gave Hope and Tianna debilitating bouts with diarrhea.

I had called Sammy the day before New Year's, hoping he could give me some advice.

His response: "Since when is your wife in charge of your career?"

"She's not," I said. "But for some reason I feel kind of obligated to at least try."

"Hey, I understand. You just got married. You want to make her happy."

"Definitely. And you know, a year ago I wouldn't have cared if I got fired, but now I actually like my job. And I'd certainly miss seeing you every week."

"Well someone's gonna miss you being around here too. That kid who writes on the window has written 'Where's

Jack?' almost every day you been gone. Looks like you gotta fan club."

"Seriously?"

"I'll be honest with you, Jack, I don't want a new guy, but you gotta do what you gotta do. Don't be a stranger though, you hear?" Sammy hung up quickly.

When my boss at the paper heard I wasn't coming back he said, "There's not much I can do. Call us when you're ready to come back, but I can't make any promises." Then, as he was hanging up he said, "Do me a favor and call Sammy." Another pause. "Are you sure you can't come back?"

"Not for a few months."

"Hhm . . . No, that's just too long. Call Sammy and explain, alright? Please?"

"I already did. He'll be waiting for your call."

"Would a raise change your mind?"

"I wish it was that simple."

Flying home our pilot was happy to announce the U.S. Olympic silver medalist in figure skating was on our plane. He congratulated her over the intercom; everyone applauded. She was sitting across the aisle but I hadn't recognized her out of sequins. The girl had recently been on the news, visiting the White House to support the president's fight against teen smoking. A teenager herself, it's doubtful she'd begun to menstruate; so determined in her quest for gold, even nature had to stop and watch.

Hope's mother gave me a book for Christmas. Her card said, "I get the feeling you don't read much . . . try this." The book, *This Boy's Life,* is about a guy's childhood, and the relationship he had with his mother and stepfather. Hope was surprised to see me so engaged and started asking questions.

"It's a good book," I said. "It makes me think about what kind of book I could write."

"A writer?" She said it sarcastically, her eyebrows raised. "All this time, I never knew."

Hope was antsy from the flight; the figure skater wasn't helping. One night in Locust Valley while Hope and her mother were in Manhattan at a musical, Tianna secretly told me about Hope's childhood dreams of being a figure skater. Sounded like Hope was pretty good, but the older and better she got, the more her mother interfered. Finally she made Hope quit, blaming the figure skating for getting in the way of her studies. Hope was only in fourth grade but had already won several state competitions. Tianna said Hope will never talk about it, with anyone, and made me promise to keep my mouth shut. Then she said, "I can't believe I just told you that. You're trouble."

Shortly following the pilot's announcement, a group of people gathered around the figure skater, asking for her autograph.

"I didn't say I was going to actually write a book."

"First no french fries, and now a novel. Tell me, Jack, do you ever tire?"

"The book made me think of Dad, that's all."

Hope was silent for a few minutes. "That's exactly what you should do. Write about your father."

"I'm calling Sammy. Hopefully, he can help me get my job back."

"Don't. Write a book instead."

"I can't live off your money."

"I know." She smiled sympathetically. "But maybe you'll be famous someday. Then I'd really have me a catch. Just try it."

Now, a day later, Hope is flipping through a continuing education catalogue while I sit at our kitchen table with two pens and a blank pad of yellow legal paper. She knows I'm stuck, and feels responsible. She walks behind me and massages my shoulders. "So where are you going to start?"

The thought of me writing a book about my father is absurd. I'd have better luck trying to get a membership at GreadeRock. But there are a few things I'd like to know: Has Dad lost his sanity? How far would he go for money? Has he been following me, and why? How much does he know about Hope? And, would anyone notice if he vanished?

My father picked me up at the airport wearing a green suit he'd bought for St. Patrick's Day. A lanky guy my age stood next to him, holding a sign that said only "Jack." Dad's tie had a flock of geese flying diagonally across the polyester. A goose cufflink accented the bottom of each shirtsleeve.

"What's with the birds?" I asked.

The lanky one, Gill, said, "Your dad is known around here as 'The Gooseman.'"

It might be true. The doorman spots us coming from the parking lot and shouts, "Look out! It's the wild goose!" A bellhop pushing a baggage cart shapes his fingers into a gun pointing at Dad. "Yo, Gooseman, don't forget about me when you lay that golden egg." Waiting for the elevator a man passes and says my father's real name once, in a grave tone.

"That's the manager," Dad says. "Good friend of mine."

The suite has an exercise bike in the corner. The walls are beige, the rug is tan, and the curtains are deep purple. Dad squeezes my neck and says, "Home sweet home. Not bad for hotel living, but I'm gonna buy a house soon." The furniture is sturdy but uncomfortable, the bed cover shiny on the outside, fuzzy underneath. The only personal belongings in the room are miniature figures from the movie *Star Wars,* lined in a row looking out the window toward the boardwalk below.

"I didn't know you were such a big *Star Wars* fan," I say, while Dad calls the front desk to check his messages.

He replaces the phone and picks up Han Solo. "No one had faith in this movie. And now, twenty years later, it's selling out theaters all over again." He begins to undress. "If you don't mind I'm gonna get on the exercycle; we can still talk while I ride."

As my dad pedals I stand by his side unsure of my next move. Looking at the middle-aged man, puffing, dressed in a silver and gold Fila sweat suit, his entire body heaving with the pedals, I don't know where, how, or why to begin. There is everything and nothing to ask this man: In most ways, I don't care about this stranger who is only my father in the technical sense of the word.

I want to say, "Dad, how much to get you off my back forever?" But what if Dad is nothing but lonely? There's no proof he's done anything but send me a few groveling letters. Dad's towel slides off the handlebars. With the assuming authority of a father he says, "Jack, can you get that for me?" and reflexively I bend, reaching for the floor obediently, not even thinking.

Hope has taken up interior design. Decorating just may be her passion; she's enrolled in a class to find out. Dad is recovering from exercise so I call her from the bedroom. Her first class was today. She said it could have been her sorority's reunion; even Dr. Reeny was there.

"What about her practice?" I ask sarcastically. "All that hard work for nothing?"

Hope doesn't like my tone. "How's the tour de force?"

"I'm almost finished. Thanks for the vote of confidence. Oh, and in case you care, Dad's great."

"Honey, I was only kidding. I have to run and look at wallpaper. See you when you get home."

Being in the same room with Dad is nothing less than bizarre. Different emotions course through my body like the quick, unpredictable flow of quarters spit from a hot slot machine. Fear, hatred, pity, and resentment. Some optimism creeps in before I have a chance to block it. I had wanted to talk to Hope about this; I needed to talk with someone about it. Breach would have been best since she knows the most about my dad, but she's moved in with her "beau" and I can't call her there. As my fingers dial the next long distance number I'm reminded of the afternoon I had called Mark's father. But this time, instead of trying to separate myself, I feel more connected than I'd like to, way more connected than I thought possible.

"Merideth, it's me, Jack."

Agitated: "What are you calling here for?"

"I'm in Atlantic City, visiting my father."

"Is he all right?"

"Depends who you ask."

"Well, are you?"

"I'm standing in a hotel room decorated with action figures my dad got with his Happy Meal. He wants me to call him Gooseman, and I know that the worst is yet to come. He's trying to look like a bigshot but I think he's doing a bad job on purpose."

"Why would he do that?"

"For sympathy, forgiveness, maybe to make me feel guilty." Actually, I think Dad's intentions are much worse.

"This is unfair; we haven't talked in months. I have no right to dump this on you. I know I shouldn't have called but I couldn't help it. I'll let you go. Sorry."

"Jack, don't hang up. Go ahead. Tell me about it." So I did and we talked for nearly an hour. Merideth listened, calmed my nerves, and gave me advice and encouragement. I apologized again for calling, acknowledging it was out of line, but she didn't mind, she was happy to listen; besides, she'd missed our talks. I told her she was special and that her husband was obviously an idiot to treat her like he did. I could hear her sniffling as she hung up the phone.

Dad has on a fresh suit: pinstriped, with a bright yellow tie bearing two black dots, side by side at the bottom. He steps out of his room, raises an arm, and says, "Tonight, we're gambling."

"Big-time, baby! Big-time!" Gill pumps his fists.

I grab the bottom of Dad's tie, "Snake eyes?"

"Goose bill."

"I wanted to bring my shirt, but it doesn't fit anymore."

Dad brushes the tie where my fingers were, "What shirt?"

"Snake-Eyed Jack. Remember?"

"Oh, yes, that one. Too bad it doesn't fit, must have shrunk." He turns to Gill, "Have you got some paper? Let's figure out breakfast."

"It didn't shrink, Dad. You gave it to me ten years ago."

Dad says, "This is what we need: orange juice, milk, more cereal, beer, and cigarettes." Gill writes on a pad of paper provided by the hotel.

Dad nods a solemn thank you to Gill. "Breakfast, Jack, is the most important meal, which is why I eat it in my room and not downstairs in the diner. Right, Gill?"

"Yes, sir. But don't be giving away all your secrets."

"He's my son, Gill, I can tell him."

"What's the big secret, that breakfast is an important meal?" I pump my fist and say, "Big-time! You guys going public with this?"

Gill takes offense and says, "It's how it's eaten."

Dad pats Gill gently on the back. "Let me explain: Jack, Thanksgiving Day the diner was serving turkey roll and stuffing at nine in the morning. I'd only gone to sleep a few hours earlier and didn't want turkey. So back in my room I ate breakfast alone, watching the parade on television. No people, machines, noise, just the tranquillity of an empty room. I won big-time that day, Jack. And I haven't stopped since."

Gill parks the car at the supermarket. To our left is a huge recycling bin. Dad turns from the front seat, "There's one more thing you should know. I call it the Freedom Clean. Basically, I say what I think, which isn't always what people want to hear."

"And this also helps you gamble better?"

Gill looks over his shoulder, "Gooseman never loses, Jack. Proof."

"It helps, Jack, because my brain doesn't have to worry about what it should or shouldn't say. I'm never distracted."

The cashier is a large man who cut the sleeves off his uniform so his muscles could fit. Taped to the counter is a flyer promoting his wrestling match. On top of his register is a short, fat calendar with a page listing a new vocabulary word for every day. The side of the register is decorated with some of the man's favorite words. *Amicable, repertoire,* and *insidious* are a few. My father minds his own business until the wrestler decides to speak. "It's not my intuitiveness to comment on the customer's habits, but your selection of breakfast foods, cigarettes, and beer strikes me as being ironical."

My father looks at the flyer with the man's picture. "This is you, right?"

"Yes sir."

"I see you wrestle under the name, Dr. Damage."

He flexes his biceps, showing a tattoo of the letters, M.D. "That's me."

"Well, Doctor, it's obvious intelligence turns you on. Let me commend you on your efforts to further your vocabulary. However, people who use big words incorrectly look less intelligent than those who use small words appropriately."

Gill holds the groceries, my father already has his change, and we could run if we had to, but there's a long line of customers waiting behind us so there isn't much the Doctor can do.

Gill puts the car in gear. "So Dad, you're going to gamble better because you insulted that man?"

Without turning around my father says, "If I said nothing, who knows how long I'd be thinking about it. Now I can concentrate on other things. Think of all the times you never said what you wanted."

"I do it all the time. It's called self-control and respecting others."

"Call it what you want, son, you're still wasting your time."

Gill takes the groceries upstairs and meets us at roulette. The floor is crowded and loud and somewhere behind us, probably at a craps table, a man shouts: *Dear Lawd, fo'get 'bout ma pass, don' worry 'bout de future, but God Awmighty, please don' leave me now!*"

Dad hits almost every number. Gill says he's just warming up, then turns to Dad and shouts, "Just like that night in Vegas, eh Gooseman?" But Dad pretends not to hear him, which is strange because why wouldn't the Gooseman want to brag about a big night in Vegas?

Craps is next. Gooseman's got a favorite table. We drink tequila sunrises, calling out numbers and giving nicknames to the other players, making almost everyone winners with the rolls of our dice. With both hands Dad pushes all his chips to one number. He hands me the dice and says, "Let 'em ride."

I throw the dice up and out the way a person flings a life preserver. My arm stretches and stays extended, wrist cocked, fingers curled in a neat row. The dice take one bounce and fly off the end of the table with a disappointing moan from the crowd.

A man with a gold, plastic name tag pulls the dice back with a miniature hoe.

Dad grabs them saying, "Maybe we should stick to the old system." Then, just as he has all night, and presumably since he discovered breakfast alone and unrestrained truth, he walks away with it. Gooseman once again denies his vulnerability to the consequences of the dice.

I leave the following day. Gill drives me to the airport after a bowl of cereal with Dad.

"I hear you hit the jackpot with your new wife. If I were you I'd keep her on a short leash."

"That so?"

"Your dad's a good man. He's doing alright now, but life ain't always so great. You should think about him sometime."

Sarcastically: "You learning a lot from him, Gill?"

"Why'd you come here anyway kid?"

Dad wasn't known as the Gooseman. The guys at the door called him that once, earning whatever bill he had slipped them along with instructions. The dressers in the suite were empty, as were the cabinets in the bathroom. A suitcase tucked in the corner of his closet had a few extra *Star Wars* figures, and a clean pair of underwear. Dad ate his cereal the way a child is forced to eat spinach, and the rush he felt to get checked out of the suite was obvious. It would be nice to know if Gill is getting paid for his role now, or if he's working toward a bigger payoff.

"Does my dad owe anybody money, Gill? Is he in a lot of debt?"

"To the best of my knowledge: he's clean."

"You ever been out West, Gill?"

"Does West Virginia count?"

"What about Dad? Does he ever leave town?"

"Does the county jail count?"

Dr. Reeny's waiting at the gate in the airport back home. She's boarding my plane, heading west to California. She's wearing a sundress, anticipating the weather in San Diego. A stack of glossy magazines are under one arm, her other hand holds a tennis racket. The frame is metallic silvery-blue, bubble-shaped and twice as wide as normal. The strings are neon-pink, in an oversized head.

"That's some racket you've got," I tell her.

"You like?" She says, twisting it.

"On your way to a psychology conference?" I grab her racket and pat the strings against my palm. "How's it going with your patients? Or is that confidential?"

"I probably shouldn't say."

The Gooseman would take one look at her and say, "I doubt you even know how to spell psychology. You probably think Freud is the newest J Crew color."

Handing back the racket I agree. "Sometimes it's best to say nothing."

My suitcase slides down the rollers onto the slowly rotating claim. I take it to an empty section of seats, putting down the bag when a person squeezes my sides from behind and says, "Gotcha!"

Caught off guard, I stumble forward, trip over my bag, and bring my assailant down with me. The body on top of me giggles until we both hear a little girl say, "Look Mom, they're in love."

Merideth climbs off. "Sorry. I didn't mean to knock you over. I thought you'd need a ride. Hope's not here, is she?"

"No, it's alright. You didn't have to pick me up, though."

"It's probably a mistake, but I couldn't help myself. You didn't sound so good on the phone."

Hope gets home late from a field trip. Her design class took a tour of open houses in a ritzy neighborhood. They ate tiny sandwiches and drank cranberry juice while being lectured on ambience and how to create moods.

In the morning she's loudly making coffee; the sink runs longer than normal; a pan drops to the floor. At the top of the stairs a stack of unconstructed cardboard boxes lean against the living room couch.

"What's all this?" I say, half awake.

"Those are for when we move."

"That's funny, I don't remember us talking about a move."

My savings account is empty. Hope wrote the last rent

check herself. Tomorrow Sammy will watch me beg. Hopefully, my replacement is incompetent.

"I've been meaning to talk to you, Jack." Hope hands me her coffee. "I've been living here a long time. I'm tired of paying rent; it's a waste of money."

"And now that I'm not splitting it with you."

"It's not that. I just think if we move into our own house it'll look better. More *permanent*."

"Are you ever going to stop listening to your mother?"

"Believe me, Jack, the only way my buying a house will please my mother is if I do it in Locust Valley. This place is small, we're gonna have to move when we have kids anyway."

Gooseman's Freedom Clean flashes. "I'm not having kids with you."

"Jack?"

"We're too young. Period. I know you're the one paying the bills, but I get a voice in some decisions."

"Honey, relax. I was talking about the future, not tomorrow. Besides, I told you not to worry about money."

"Well, I'm going back to work."

"Don't. Really." She rubs my shoulders. "What about your writing?" she asks as if I've been slaving behind a typewriter every day of my life.

"The one thing about gambling," Dad had said, "is that you gotta know when to stop." Gill stuck his chin out and nodded. Where could those two have met? Probably at the slot machines talking percentage and averages. Dad projected himself as a winner; Gill didn't buy it, but hung around anyway, either for the company, the lure of a long shot, or maybe because every young man wants guidance.

Sammy's gonna feed me some crow. First I'll get the cold–New York–shoulder, then he'll raise his voice asking me what he's *supposed to do here.* I can feel the shame already, but then he'll get cerebral, eyes on the floor, and tell me I'm a *good kid.*

I'll look at him and say, "Sammy, you don't know how grateful I am."

And he won't.

battleship

Merideth agreed to meet me at the coffee shop, but there was hesitation in her voice and she made it clear that she wouldn't stay for long. Hope is in Aspen with the Locust Valley Five. Alden's father has a ski mansion there—both a sound real estate investment and an excellent redecoration project for his current trophy wife. Hope had invited me but didn't seem too upset when I explained that celebrities, Wall Street moguls, and twangy Texans aren't my scene.

"I knew you'd say something like that," she said. "I guess we'll just have to have fun without you."

"Don't drink too much."

"You're so smug, you know that? I don't know why you think you're so much better than them."

"I'm only trying to warn you about the altitude. Liquor goes straight to your head up there."

"I'm not stupid, Jack."

She's not. She knew the reason I didn't want to go was because she'd be paying, and that I didn't really believe in vacations for the unemployed. She said to me later that day, "Jack, I know you quit your job for me, and I feel really bad, but come to Aspen. We'll have a good time. It's silly to get hung up about money."

I had just gotten back from Atlantic City and told her I wanted to get settled and gather some thoughts before getting on my knees in front of Sammy. I was also worried about the Gooseman's next move. Going skiing for the weekend seemed like a bad idea.

"I understand," Hope said. Then she took off her wedding ring and handed it to me. "Watch this for me while I'm gone, will you? The altitude makes your fingers swell, I might not be able to get it off once I'm there."

"Why don't you take mine then, it's bigger."

She laughed, put her ring back on, and asked me to get her skis out of storage. Since our wedding Hope seems to have lost interest in our being a couple. She behaves like a person who has made his or her point and won't listen to any more arguments.

Merideth finds my table and sits down across from me. She doesn't take off her sunglasses. "So where's your wife?"

"She's catching the end of the ski season. I didn't feel like taking a trip she was paying for."

"Is she giving you a hard time about that?"

"No. Actually, I think she's enjoying it. A little too much."

Merideth puts her elbows on the table. "So Jack, what do you want from me?"

"I wanted to thank you for coming to the airport."

"When you told me you were getting married and we'd have to stop seeing each other, that was fine. I respect your decision. But you have to respect my feelings as well, and not call me whenever it strikes your fancy."

"It was a mistake to call you from Atlantic City. I'm sorry, I was having a hard time."

"You can't have it both ways, Jack. I'm not some light switch you can turn on and off."

"So, why did you pick me up at the airport?"

"Well maybe I had a weak moment too, which is exactly my point. In the time we've known each other I've already exposed too much of myself. I refuse to care about someone unavailable. Believe me, I've had enough of that for one lifetime."

I asked her, "Don't you think I care about you?" With Hope acting aloof and Breach no longer available, I'll admit part of my attachment to Merideth is purely out of need, but the night I called her from Atlantic City meant a lot to me. She made herself available that night with no selfish motivations and that's exactly what she's done all along.

"Maybe I'm an idiot, but yes."

"Good. And maybe I'm an idiot too, but I definitely think you care about me."

"You're not an idiot."

"Well I like the way that feels, and I don't always get that from Hope."

"You're gonna have to work that out with her then."

"You're right. I know. But sometimes I think I'd rather work it out with you."

"Jack, where do you think this could go? I'm almost forty years old; I have two kids. We have no future. Period."

She'd never before told me her age and it was a bit of a shock. I would have guessed she could be no older than thirty-five. "I know, I know. But when you don't have a lot of people who care about you, it's hard to give one of them up."

After Breach's semi-nasty email about missing her Last Call I phoned her and we had this rather brief conversation:

ME: You know when we broke up, it wasn't because I was holding out for something better, I just wasn't ready to get so serious.

HER: And now you're married.

ME: Right.

HER: So, you were ready to get serious, just not with me.

ME: I wasn't with you when I got married.

HER: Exactly.

ME: Are you trying to make this difficult?

HER: Are you finding this difficult?

ME: Yes.

HER: Well so am I.

And she hung up.

Merideth is getting more and more upset as we talk. "Jack, you said it yourself a few months ago, 'It was impractical in the first place, and now that I'm getting married, it's even more so.'"

She's quoting me exactly and it's hard to say whether she's just got a good memory, or if pain made the words stick.

"After Atlantic City, I guess I just realized how valuable a friend you are."

"I'm glad I could help, but it stops here. I don't need a friend, especially one that can hurt me."

She walked me to my car and saw my Snake-Eyed Jack shirt in the back seat. Hope had asked me to throw it out but I hadn't been ready to part with it yet.

Staring at the shirt Merideth said, "You never told me your nickname was Snake-Eyed Jack."

"My dad gave me that a long time ago."

"It's hideous."

"Want it?"

"Your dad gave you that shirt. I can't take it."

"Please," I said. "Take it. There's just one catch . . . You have to promise you'll wear it. Think of it as something to remember me by."

She held the shirt in front of her face, trying not to cringe. She kissed me on the cheek and said, "Give it time, Jack. Things sometimes have a way of working themselves out." She thought a moment, possibly about herself, and frowned before saying, "Don't let your whole life go by, though."

I reached to remove her sunglasses so that I could look her in the eye one more time as I thanked her. She flinched so hard her glasses slipped off revealing a bruised left eye. In a panic, she reached down for her glasses. Then she froze.

"Your husband?" I said.

She shook her head and said, "Just don't call me anymore, okay Jack?" Then she turned and walked away.

Sammy's windows are dark, a message is written in large letters along the entire bottom width of the fifteen-foot glass. The words are printed neatly: SUPER JACK WHERE YA BEEN? TWO FOR ONE SPECIAL, GRASS IS ALWAYS GREENER, OR IS IT, MARRY—DEATH? Taped on the inside of the door is a note. "Closed. Business back home. Please try again the first of next month." Inside, the lights are off and the refrigerated cases empty. Around back his dumpster is locked shut with a thickly linked chain, coiled through the lid's handle. As I'm getting napkins next door the cashier looks at me like, "Where've you been?" I raise a hand, "Thanks," and go to work on Sammy's windows.

monopoly

Neither of us says a word in the elevator. She unlocks the door to an unlit apartment and leads me by the hand to her mother's bedroom. She turns a lamp on low and slips her dress over her head saying, "Do you need a drink?"

"What's going on?"

"I'm going to bed."

"Then why did you bring me here?"

"Oh Jack, do I really have to explain?"

"Yeah, I think you do. You're my wife's best friend."

Hope doesn't like it when I use her coffee machine. Her mother bought it in Italy. This is Hope's second. I broke the first, three days after it arrived, snapping the handle off a removable filter. Hope hinted at sabotage.

"Why would I want to ruin your coffee machine?"

She cradled the broken grip in her palm the way a little girl holds the splintered egg of a blue jay. "Because it's fancy."

A few weeks after our engagement a shipment arrived containing an assortment of Hope's more valuable belongings. Some of the things she had to explain.

"Jack, you're marrying me. You better get used to the fact that I have money. There are worse fates, you know."

Today we're looking at houses. Hope has already warned me about more new arrivals once we find a place. All kinds of tables and couches from a country house her grandfather used to own. Hope doesn't know I enjoy her furniture. She still believes her stuff makes me uncomfortable. In reality, the adjustment was quite simple.

"She doesn't love you, Jack." Tianna slips her shoes off with each opposite foot's big toe, leaving nothing on her body but a black set of lingerie. The bed's got maybe twelve pillows, four rows of three, smallest up front and so on. She drunkenly swats six off with one shove. I'm still standing at the foot of the bed. She walks on her knees to the edge and sits on her heels, waiting for an answer.

"She married me, didn't she? Don't you think that means something?"

"I know exactly what it means."

"Then tell me."

Tianna pulls my wrist, sitting me next to her. "Oh, sweetheart," she scratches the inside of my arm. "You don't really want to know, do you?"

We meet the real estate agent outside her office. Cassandra's gregarious nature is consistent with her curvy body and chosen vocation of sales. She tells us to call her Cass, and introduces her daughter, Constance. Constance is taller than Cass, but they share the same beautiful face, exotic in an unplaced, foreign way. A recent college grad, Constance is training to join her mother in the world of real estate sales. Cassandra tells her to ride with me in the back seat of the car.

The first house belongs to a local celebrity, Dealin' Dan.

He owns car dealerships throughout the area, selling everything from foreign to domestic, luxury to economy. His advertisements dominate the thirty-second slots devoted to local businesses. The ads are hilarious. Low budget affairs that succeed by mocking the very lack of thought and investment put into their creation. He stars in all of them, dressed up as Superman, Zorro, and, my favorite, a space alien promising prices "out of this world."

His house is modern, painted white with lots of large glass windows facing the mountains. On moving day Dan's wife and children never appeared, but instead, migrated to another state. Mrs. Dealin' Dan had a deal of her own with the moving company, paying them double to keep her plans secret. Cassandra says it was Dan's workaholism. No one blamed his wife; Dan's reaction was to go back to his office and work.

"It's so sad," Cassandra frowns. "Look at this house, you'd think it would be enough."

Cass and Hope begin to inspect the details of every room so Constance and I sit outside on the porch furniture. Fully reclined in the sun, with her eyes shut Constance says, "I could get used to this job."

"Is this your first day?"

"Yeah. I'm a little worried about working for Mom, but it should be alright."

"Did your school have a good real estate program?"

"I was a political science major."

"Oh, well, real estate agents need to be good politicians too, I guess."

She snickers. "That's exactly what Mom said."

A sliding door opens, Cass calls for Constance, Hope takes her place in the sun.

"My furniture back home is perfect for this place. Mom's gonna love it. What do you think?"

"Sounds like you already made up your mind."

"I'm supposed to believe you, sitting there in your underwear, trying to seduce me? This is sick, Tianna."

"You and I are one and the same, Jack. Do you know why Alden married me?" She moves off her heels and straightens one leg behind my back, the other across my lap.

"Yeah, but I don't have any money."

She reaches for my hands and holds them between her legs. "I'll say this, the circumstances of my marriage weren't only driven by love, nor were yours."

"Then why'd you say yes? And Hope too, for that matter?"

She shuts her eyes and sighs a deep breath, lowering her arms so my fingers touch the highest part of her thighs. "Did you hear what I just said?"

I pull my hands away, crossing my arms. "I don't believe you."

"Remember when she cried on your honeymoon, Jack?"

The houses are built in perfect rows, each with a manicured lawn, all on one side of a road that weaves a giant circle in a roundabout sort of way. The inside of the circle is a park with a playground, playing field, and shallow lake. Cassandra drives slowly over the road's speed bumps and parks in front of a yellow house with a white picket fence. She pulls Hope and me aside before we enter.

"Now, Jack. This house isn't going to be nearly as spectacular as Dealin' Dan's," she actually calls him Dealin' Dan. "But I can't think of a better place for two young people to raise a family."

"That's really good to know, Cassandra. Thank you for informing me."

We start to walk toward the front door. I grab the back of Hope's shirt, *"Raise a family?* What the hell was that?"

"I don't know. She's a real estate agent, that's probably her angle. You know how sketchy salespeople can be."

"I used to be one, remember? By the way, what would your mom think about us having kids? I'd be curious to know."

"Why don't you ask her yourself then."

"Maybe I'll call her when we get home."

"My mom can't wait for me to have kids. A grandchild is the perfect way for her to meddle in my life."

Mrs. Johnson opens the door. Her eyes are red and puffy, her hair combed in a hurry. She's wearing blue jeans and a baggy sweater with the last name of a trendy designer written in big letters across the front. She looks a few years older than thirty, and invites us in, apologizing for the mess.

The house isn't all that messy. The living room's dark blue carpet appears to have been vacuumed just seconds prior to our arrival. In one corner a wicker basket of toys looks like it's about to topple over and take with it a crooked stack of board games. Their couch is light brown. One of the arms was doodled on by an inexpert hand with a black, permanent marker. Folded next to the other arm is a blanket and bed pillow.

Off the living room is a dining room carpeted with the same blue rug. The only furniture is a table with protective plastic covers stuck over the corners. The kitchen has a speckled linoleum floor; the cabinets have childproof locks.

Upstairs there are three bedrooms off one hall. One room has a racing car bed and posters of baseball players, the other has a crib filled with dolls. In the master bedroom the bed has been made except for one missing pillow.

"People cry when they're happy."

Tianna throws her head back in disgust, moaning. "The happiest person at your wedding was Hope's mother, and she wasn't crying."

"Hope's mother hates me—"

"—Hope's mother is always one step ahead of Hope. The second you guys break up Hope's gonna need her even more, which is exactly what her mother wants."

"Well I got bad news for you, Tianna. Hope and I won't be breaking up anytime soon."

Tianna tilts her head and smiles condescendingly.

"What makes you so confident?"

She tightens her smirk into a serious expression. "Girls like Hope and I, we're all made from the same cookie cutter, Jack. For life. Hope will be back in Locust Valley sooner than she thinks." Her smile returns, "Buying a house isn't going to solve anything."

Hope, Cass, and Constance have gone to see the playground. Cass picked up immediately that Hope didn't like the house and continues to stress the importance of surroundings. Downstairs Mrs. Johnson is cleaning the kitchen windows.

"So why are you moving?" I ask.

Her eyes swell. "My husband," she says, then grabs a tissue and blows her nose.

"Sorry. It's none of my business."

"There's just a lot to think about." She pulls an orange crayon from behind a sugar jar and quickly leaves the room.

Cass tells Hope about the community's Monday night

picnic. Hope rolls her eyes and smiles secretly at me. "Actually, Cass, do you think we could go back to Dealin' Dan's?"

We can't leave the Johnsons' fast enough. Our car rolls slowly over speed bump after speed bump, yellow warning signs with black silhouettes of children give the entire area a feeling of heightened caution.

At Dan's the bright white tiles and extensive panes of glass give a clean, sterile atmosphere. Hope stands beneath the center of the raised triangle roof, spins once with her arms stretched out, and says, "I'll take it."

"What are you trying to tell me? I wish you'd just say it so I could get out of here."

Tianna tries to loosen one of my crossed arms, "You're not gonna want to leave after hearing what I have to say."

Hope comes home with the mail. "Something came for you." She hands me an envelope with a plane ticket inside.

"You bought me a plane ticket?"

"You could say thank you."

"Thanks," I say. "What's the occasion and where am I going?"

"There's no occasion. I thought you might want to see your friends in New York. I'm trying to be nice."

"What about the house? We're moving Saturday." Hope, Dealin' Dan, and Cassandra were all happy to rush the paperwork. "Don't you want me around for that?"

"My mother's coming tomorrow. It actually works out well. Her plane lands an hour before yours takes off."

Looking at the ticket I see that my seat is booked in Business Class. "Business Class? Good to see I'm moving up in the world."

"That's all they had."

"You know, we're moving into this house together. I wouldn't mind helping. I'd actually kind of like to. It is our first house."

Hope smiles, hugging me. "Oh Jack, that's sweet of you. But Mom'll be here. We'll be fine without you. Go have fun in New York."

"I know your mother doesn't like me, but I promise to be civil. I swear."

"Jack, it'll be easier for everyone, including you. Go have some fun."

"Fun would be seeing you tell your mother off, and that if she doesn't want to accept us, she can just stay in Long Island."

"My mom has to help me, Jack. It's my first house. Shutting her out would be like not letting her plan my wedding."

Tianna wraps her leg around my waist and knocks me over. "If you really want to know, Hope's trust fund requires that she get married before she gets all of her money."

I get off the bed and sit on a couch in the dark part of the room. Tianna flips over from her stomach. She arches her back and unbunches her underwear.

From the dark I say, "Hope already had plenty of money. She said 'I do' because she loves me."

Tianna comes over to the couch, grabs her purse from the floor, and takes out a scarf to get to her pack of cigarettes.

"That looks like the scarf that the girl was wearing at the table next to us."

"That's because it is, Jack. The money Hope got from her

trust makes her even wealthier than her mother. Neither of them is going to starve, but it gives Hope that psychological advantage."

"I can't believe you stole that girl's scarf."

"Don't worry Jack, her father owns half of Greenwich. She certainly won't miss an Hermès scarf."

"You know her?"

"We came out together. But even if Hope had all the money in the world, it wouldn't matter. Her mother's forgiveness isn't for sale."

At the airport the next day Hope's mother is the first person off the plane. She gives Hope a big hug then explains she's *horribly* thirsty, and asks Hope to get her a bottle of Evian at a newsstand down the terminal. Hope is reluctant until her mother pulls a large manila envelope from her purse and says, "Just give us a minute, darling."

When Hope leaves she hands me the envelope, which contains copies of the papers I signed at her Christmas party. "These are for your own records, Jack. Thanks again for your cooperation."

"No problem. You're gonna like the house. Hope did a good job picking it out."

Without warning she grabs my wrist and yanks me behind a bank of payphones. "I must say, Jack," her voice is half sultry, half evil. "I'm upset we won't be spending the night under the same roof. I've been looking forward to it." She's a very attractive woman; there's no doubt this approach has gotten her a lot of what she's wanted.

"You really must think I'm an idiot, don't you?"

She lifts up my arm and gives my hand a wet kiss. "Not at

all. Hope knows she owes me. We've talked about it, Jack. She's okay with it as long as you are."

With mock excitement, "Really? Gosh!" Then sarcastically, "And this whole time I thought you were trying to set me up."

She lets go of my wrist.

"See these papers?" I hold them up to her face. "They're proof of something very real, understand?"

"Of course I do, Jack." She laughs, flipping her hair back casually. "Why *else* would I have you sign them?"

"Your life is so empty you need to wield power where you don't belong. You blame your husband's death on Hope and you torture her to get even."

Her hand comes sideways toward my face but this time it's me grabbing her wrist. I stop her slap short. "But look at it this way Ms. Witherspoon, marriages last a long time so we'll have another shot at spending the night together *real* soon." I tuck the papers in my back pocket, turning to find my departure gate.

As I walk away I can hear her laughing, saying, "Don't count on it," then laughing again.

Tianna lifts me off the bed. She rests her hands on my shoulders, gives a sympathetic frown, and starts to unbutton my shirt. "I got used too, but at least I knew while it was happening. Now you know. Use this information. Use her back."

I turn away from her, rebuttoning my shirt.

In a deadpan voice she asks, "What did Hope say about our trip to Aspen?"

"She said you had fun and that Sonny Wingwright broke his arm trying to learn how to snowboard after a few drinks."

"She didn't mention that we saw James Kidder?"

Annoyed with Tianna and our conversation I sigh and say, "No."

"Just like your honeymoon. Quite a coincidence, wouldn't you say?"

The cab driver taking me from LaGuardia into Manhattan wears a T-shirt that says, "If ignorance is bliss, why aren't more people happy?" Before going out my friends and I drink a case of beer while watching hockey on television. The game ends around eleven. Tianna's at the same bar with some girls I've never met before. Her black cocktail dress looks so flimsy it might fray into pieces if I tug hard enough. My friends are disappointed to find out she's married, but Alden is in Aspen doing community service for a DWI. We sit at a large round table, my friends are happy to get acquainted with Tianna's circle. Tianna follows me to the bar to get another round of drinks.

"I need to talk to you, Jack. In private."

"Now?"

"Later. Walk me home tonight and I'll explain."

Hope makes me shut my eyes at the front door. Opening them reveals wooden tables and trunks from the turn of the century mixed with colorfully schemed couches and armchairs. Tall hutches filled with pottery accent corners. Antique posters decorate the walls. The replacement coffee machine rests stoically overlooking a spotless kitchen.

"What do you think?" She bites her lip, pulls a chair from a table then pushes it back. In all of Hope's meticulousness lurks a silent unrest, a discontent, that asks, "What could possibly be missing?"

Upstairs in our bedroom the Buddha Hope still doesn't

know Breach gave me is tucked in the corner of a bookcase, my only belonging underneath this roof, asking, "What's not missing?"

Many drinks and a few hours later the bar closes. Tianna grabs my hand under the table and says, "Let's get out of here. We need to talk about Hope."

Our friends don't seem to care we won't be joining them. A few jokes about married life are made as we wave goodnight through the window of a cab.

Tianna gives the address of her mother's Park Avenue apartment and sits back, putting her hand on my knee. Under the awning of her building I tell her it's getting late but she clasps her hands around the back of my neck, looks directly into my face, and sounding the most sober she has all night says, "You're your own person, aren't you, Jack?"

Boredom sets in on the flight home. For reading material I choose the papers from Hope's mother. The legal text is confusing, a secret language to those outside the practice. But what's clear is my half-drunken signature at the bottom of every page, and next to each one, the precisely written number 2, correcting the previously marked date, no longer matching the day following Hope's own cursively drawn name. I may not be the lawyer Hope's mother wants me to be, but I know that if this prenuptial contract were ever threatened to be contested in a court of law, a large settlement would be offered to keep things tidy. And just like the Gooseman taught me: I'd know when to quit.

My Business Class flying partner, a man seeming to be a veteran of travel, asks me what I do for a living, curious not so much about my occupation, as how I managed to end up in the leather seat next to him. I lie, saying I'm in the news-paper business.

"You gotta be on top of things in that line of work," he says.

"Certainly," I say, looking down at the xeroxed contract. "It's all about acquiring and controlling information."

my rules

A man called for Hope. His voice was familiar but I couldn't place it and he refused to leave a name. He gave me a phone number but all I could write was, *Your world is coming to an end.*

Dad's sanity plagues me. My aunt truly believed she was the Queen of England; Dad may truly believe he's the Gooseman. His most recent letter said, *"Lady luck is smiling, Gooseman is growing wings. Get in touch soon, son; I'll be landing at your door."* The letter was forwarded from our old address.

My experience in New York with Tianna will remain a secret. Hopefully my silence will keep her as an ally. I'd ask Hope if she got more money by tying the knot, but even if it's true, Hope could have married anyone. If all Hope wanted was the rest of her trust fund, then she could have avoided a lot of torment by getting hitched to a suitable country club boy.

I believe in Hope's love for me and I admire her struggle to balance the two worlds of Locust Valley and Us. But is she balancing, or just trying to keep the two separate? Why *did* she cry on our honeymoon? What are her *real* reasons for keeping her mother and me apart? She lied about Dr. Reeny. What else is she lying about?

But now I have leverage: A tainted prenup that could

prove to be very valuable. An insurance plan I can cash at any time. A con man's dream. But this isn't a con; it's a marriage. And I'm not a con man, just a guy who happened to marry well.

Maybe I should call Breach and see what she thinks.

ouija

The man wearing a police uniform sitting in the car parked down the street is not a cop. I know this because he's my father. His current disguise is as deceiving as the bit part he played as Gooseman. He probably bought the dark navy uniform shirt at a thrift shop, but like a final five-dollar chip at the end of an unlucky streak, it's all he's got to bet on. At one point he got out of his car to stretch, succumbing to the grueling rigors of a stakeout, revealing legs paler than the underside of a shark, barely covered by a floral bathing suit and flip-flops (like father like son).

Hope doesn't know he's her father-in-law. She thinks he's Neighborhood Watch, and wants to bring him lemonade. Cassandra did not mention security; Hope is ecstatic. "He's free, Jack. Free security, isn't that great?"

I'm looking at Dad through shut blinds. "It's superb," I say, smiling.

We're in the middle of a heat wave. It hasn't rained for three weeks; the forecast shows no signs of relief. These severe weather conditions aren't just affecting our state, but the whole country. Meteorologists are baffled. The Farmer's Almanac provides no explanation. People are getting desperate. Southwestern Indians perform rain dances. Evange-

lists hold mass prayer sessions in the Plain States for the suf-
fering cattle. And while the Stock Exchange teeters, all of
Florida is aflame.

Dad must be dying. His car is black, marinating in the
sun, but unlike a casino, cool air and fresh oxygen aren't
being pumped in every fifteen minutes. His secondhand
shirt, undoubtedly unwashed, has got to itch, but worst of
all—no bets to make. I don't know what he wants exactly,
and I'm wondering how long before he takes action.

Hope is better than ever. She's been in a steady good
mood, and she quit smoking at the same time. Her mother
calls daily. Quick mysterious conversations. Hope either
leaves the room or speaks in what can only be code.

Our yard hasn't fared so well. The grass has turned brit-
tle; the soil is as hard as cement. No watering allowed. City
officials have requested severe energy conservation measures
so that hospitals and businesses can operate normally. We
keep our shades down. That's why we didn't see our neighbor's dog. It's doubtful the pup could have been saved anyway. Rabid from the heat, he must have stumbled into our
driveway and collapsed on the baking cobblestones. His
owners literally had to peel the little body off the ground.
They still have no idea how the dog got outside.

Everyone has become hermits. The streets are always
empty. Supermarkets echo at noon like it's four in the morning. Local factories have stopped daytime shifts and there's
talk about power blackouts until sunset. Even the mystery
marker has halted. I've been going by Sammy's early in the
morning to check his windows. Sammy is still out of town.

Dad worries me. Judging by the overhead of a plane
ticket, rental car, and used police shirt, this could be his
biggest gamble yet. Hope has filled a thermos with ice and

powdered lemonade. She doesn't understand why I won't carry refreshments to our neighborhood watchman.

"It's hot out there, Jack. The poor guy's probably boiling."

"They're trained for this kind of thing. Leave him alone."

She looks at me like I'm an asshole, and heads outside.

Returning she says, "What a nice man. I asked if he was security and he said, 'That I am,' then asked if I'd seen any suspicious goings-on."

Sleeping has been out of the question. Besides the heat, Hope has kept us both awake with her relentless urges to make love. Last night we had just finished. Lying on sweat-dampened sheets I felt her hand creeping down my chest.

"You gotta be kidding," I said.

"No joke. "

"It's too hot."

"Never."

"Did the doctor give you some new kind of pill or something?" She giggled in a demonic, sultry way. It could be the new bedroom, or the fact that we've been cooped inside for so long, but something has possessed her.

Tianna called. She said, "Hello Jack, can I talk to Hope?" I handed the phone over and watched.

They chatted.

After a while Hope hung up. "Tianna's pissed you went to New York and didn't call her."

"Was I supposed to?"

"I guess it would have been nice."

"Tell her next time I promise to get in touch."

Tianna's silence is a safe bet. That night in New York I ended up sleeping in a guest room in her mother's apartment. When Tianna finally accepted that I wouldn't sleep with her, she said, "You really aren't like us."

To that I replied, "And damn proud of it."

Tianna smirked and said, "Do you know what I meant when I said Hope and I are from the same cookie cutter?"

"Sorry, Tianna, you and Hope are nothing alike."

"We're the same, Jack. We're the same product, from the same mold, and not only are we expected to live the same kind of life, but deep down it's what we want, because ultimately Jack, *it's all we know.*"

"I'm going to sleep."

"Hope loves you, Jack. And if she could have it her way, she'd keep her little life with you in the mountains. But no one's gonna let that happen. Not her mom, not her friends, and not even Hope."

She was right. This morning Hope's mother called after another late night. They talked for thirty seconds. Afterwards I said, "Did you tell her you stayed up past your bedtime?"

Hope stopped in her tracks. "What the fuck is that supposed to mean?"

"She's called you every day. Exactly how vicariously does she want to live?"

"Do you want to know the truth? Because you won't like it."

"Try me."

"Well, she calls and says, 'Divorced yet?' when I answer."

"I think that falls under the category of child abuse."

"You should be flattered because I'm doing all this for you." She sat on the couch and started massaging her temples.

Sitting next to her I said, "Is there anything I can do?"

All she said back was, "I've been thinking about that."

I thought about calling the police to let them know that one of their finest has been parked on our street for the past couple days, but when I peeked out the window he was gone.

•   •   •

The six o'clock news says rain is coming. States farther west have already received the blessing. Now we must wait. Tonight, for the first time, Hope isn't interested in sex.

"Is it that time of the month?" I ask.

"Don't be gross."

After some mental calculation I say, "I guess it is, isn't it?"

The humming fan has gotten to me, neither side of my pillow is cool, and Hope is snoring. I'm getting water in the kitchen, and lightning strikes. It's so startling I drop my glass. I open the fridge door for light and step backwards onto a splintered shard. My scream echoes through the house. I hop across the kitchen floor toward the light switch.

I lean against the stove to inspect my foot; the silence following my cry is broken by a strange tapping noise from upstairs. Pausing to listen, I hear the tapping sounds grow faster on the other side of the house, then louder from both sides. Within seconds the windows are clattering with the sound of rain.

Upstairs, Hope is missing. Water breezes its way through our screened windows. From behind, the bathroom door creaks slowly open, casting a long shadow toward the bed.

A voice says, "Where've you been?"

Turning around I'm relieved to see Hope and not someone else. "Water."

"Will you get me some? I don't feel well."

"It's raining," I say.

"I know."

"What's wrong with you?"

She grimaces, shaking her head, "Yuck."

I hand her my drink. "Go back to sleep, it's late."

Walking downstairs I try to put as little weight on my heel

as possible. My heel stings with every step, even the stickiness of the bandage hurts. In the morning little dots of blood blink through the house's white carpet.

Hope is not distressed by my trail of DNA, and even less worried about our empty bedroom downstairs. An enormous crack in the wall leaked last night. The rain still hasn't stopped. We now have a six-foot-long fissure resembling a lightning bolt, and a very wet rug.

Hope passes on coffee, which she never does, and calls Cassandra, who calls Dealin' Dan, who calls us with an invitation to his office. Cassandra is mystified. In all her years of selling homes never once has a previous owner responded to a problem in a house they no longer own.

I check Hope's birth control pills, which reveal no crime—the correct amounts are missing. I look in the garbage too.

Dan's office door is cracked open a few inches. Inside a nun is explaining she's afraid of the minivan donated to her church. "The headlights stay on even when they're switched off," she says.

Dan's very patient. "Daytime running lights, standard safety feature for all the new lines. Pretty soon you won't find a car that doesn't have them."

"They're no good. It's like the car has got a mind of its own. It talks too, you know? Every time I open the door."

"We can fix that for free. But there's nothing we can do about the headlights. You're just going to have to trust me, they're for your own safety."

"I don't mean to be difficult, but I'd like a different van. I'll take an older one if I have to."

The nun leaves the door open. Dan sits with his head down. On the walls are pictures of the groundbreaking ceremonies at each of Dan's dealerships. In every photo he wears the same suit and a hard hat, holding the same shovel. After a minute he looks up, "Sorry. Have you been waiting long?"

"We just got here," Hope says. "Did we interrupt?"

Dan smiles, "No. I'm trying to learn how to meditate at my desk. My life has been such a wreck lately."

His phone rings. "Really? That's great, I'm on my way." He hangs up and thinks a minute. "I'm sorry but my name just came up on the waiting list for a Buddhism class. It starts in half an hour. I'm very concerned about your house, though, so let's reschedule."

Driving home we stop at a pharmacy. Hope's stomach is bothering her. The closest drugstore is a national chain with automatic doors and aisles like a supermarket. Everything is on sale—magazines, makeup, children's toys, tobacco. The actor from our honeymoon, James Kidder, is on the cover of a prominently displayed magazine. The picture is a close-up of his face, his left eye winking. Hope stops walking and stares at the magazine. She grabs onto a large wire cage containing a bunch of different colored balls, exhales a long breath, and says, "I feel funny." Then she falls into a kiddy pool, empty of water, but fully inflated.

Fortunately she stands right up, and though stunned, says she is fine. I walk her to the car and go back inside to buy her some medication. Waiting in line a voice behind me says, "Is Hope all right?"

"Merideth! My God, how are *you?*"

She hears what I say but blocks it out completely. "What's wrong with Hope?"

"She hasn't been feeling like herself lately. Is it normal to faint when you're pregnant?"

"She's pregnant?"

"I don't know."

"You must have worked things out after we talked."

"Actually, I've done more observing than talking. It's been a confusing month," I mutter, staring out the window. Outside in the lot Dad has parked next to our car and is talking to Hope. They both laugh; then he drives away.

Driving home, Hope offers little insight to her collapse. "Guess what?" she says. "I saw the security guard when you were getting my stuff. He saw you walk me to the car and asked if I was all right."

Hope calls her physician, and because of a cancellation, gets an appointment right away. I head to Sammy's. The deli's open, but Sammy's still gone. A guy named Jimmy introduces himself as a cousin. He's from Jersey, thirty years old and already in love with every woman who came into the shop today. He steps from behind the counter wearing a hockey shirt and hospital scrubs cut off at the knees.

"Are you Jack, as in Jack from the paper?"

"How'd you know?"

"Sammy talks about you all the time; you're always coming by to clean the windows, right?"

"Sometimes. Where is Sammy anyway?"

"It's too hot for the old man; he's visiting family."

"I really need to ask him a question."

"Try me."

"My wife is trying to get pregnant behind my back."

Jimmy makes an O with his lips. "Hhm. Maybe you should wait for Sammy." He takes two sodas from a fridge by the register and hands me one. "You could always pull out."

"We just got married."

"Not your marriage. Her."

"Either way, I think it's too late."

A customer walks in; Jimmy goes back toward the counter. "Jack, piece of advice?"

"Sure."

"Don't wait too long before you come back. Disappearing acts are for magicians."

Cassandra and an insurance agent are supposed to look at the damage caused by the rain. As I pull in the driveway Cassandra is at the front door with a midget. In a moment of clarity I can't explain, I realize that this midget is the goddamn individual who has been harassing me. So what the hell is he doing standing at our front door with our real estate agent?

Cass runs to the car. "Good news, Jack. I talked to Dan and we worked something out."

Pointing at the midget, I say, "Is he with you?"

She ignores my question. "Dan's going through a bit of a crisis right now. He's actually considering selling his dealerships."

"Really?"

"I guess the divorce was a real eye-opener. Legally he's under no obligation to repair the house, but this is a strange time in his life."

"What did he say?"

"He says he'd like to give you a car for all your troubles."

"Seriously?"

"He wants to see you this afternoon. I'd go now before he changes his mind." Cassandra heads inside to make a phone call.

The midget is with the insurance company. His name tag

says Tim. He's wearing a blue T-shirt with the Superman "S" logo. Hanging off his shoulder is a Polaroid camera. We're staring each other down.

"We haven't been formerly introduced. I'm Tim." As we begin to shake hands he grabs mine with both of his and squeezes tightly, not letting go. For such small hands he's got a firm grip and when I try to pull away he pulls back harder. "I gotta say it's a great honor to be in the presence of Super Jack, the kowtowing Mafia lover boy. What's it like running with criminals and juggling beautiful women?"

"What the hell are you talking about?"

"Haven't seen you around, Jack. Did you come to your senses and quit working for that crook Sammy, or did he fire you because you were too busy cheating on your wife?"

"Listen man, I don't know what your problem is—"

"—No you listen to me." His voice is filled with anger but lowered so that Cassandra doesn't hear him. "Guys like you make me sick, running around like you own the town, giving free business to criminals, women at your feet. You don't have the slightest clue what it's like to live a real life, Mr. Peachy-Keen."

"Do you really work for the insurance company?"

"I do now, but I used to be Tiny Tim, owner of Super Hero, until I went out of business. It's kind of hard to compete with someone who steals his merchandise."

"Yeah well, if you fuck with me again, you're gonna lose a lot more than your occupation."

"Don't threaten me, kid. You don't need me to ruin your life; turns out you can do a fine job on your own."

I step toward him. "Bullshit. You're just pissed off at the world, and you're afraid of Sammy, so you picked on me instead. Well I got a news flash for you, tomorrow Sammy's gonna find out who's been writing all over his windows, and you can expect to hear from him."

Tim comes toe to toe with me, pointing a finger at my face, about to completely lose it. Gooseman pulls up honking.

Dad leans out his window and says, "Is there a problem here?"

Tim backs away. "No problem officer."

Dad looks at me, "Do I need to get out of the car?" I shake my head, and he says, "I'll be back," before driving away.

The sight of Dad sobers my anger, so I make the following peace offer. "I'll make you a deal. Leave me alone and I won't tell Sammy about you. There's nothing you can do to stop Sammy and it's probably in your best interest not to try. I think you know this; otherwise you'd be bothering him, and not me."

Straightening his clothes Tim says, "I'll leave you alone, but I'm still gonna write on the windows."

I shake his hand once more saying, "Go ahead. I think Sammy kinda likes it."

Hope calls, and in a bubbly voice tells me Dr. Reeny is driving her home.

"Dan's giving us a car."

"Get a station wagon," she says, and hangs up.

Dan is meditating again. He looks up and sees me in his office doorway. "I can't do this," he says, shaking his head.

"You mean the car?"

He stands, points a fully extended arm, and in his television voice says, "Dealin' Dan always keeps his word, tell all your friends. It's this meditation stuff I can't handle."

"It's not for everyone."

"Certainly not me. Now come on in. I said I'd give you a car and have I got just the one for you."

Back in the swing of things, Dan tells me about a white minivan that due to a clerical error went on too many test drives, accruing so much mileage he'd have a hard time selling it as new. It's his only offer. I can take it or leave it.

I take it quick, before he gains his senses, and drive it home, leaving the Continental behind. Hope and I can pick it up later.

The house is dark and smells funny. The shades are down, light flickers from the far side of the living room, illuminating two silhouettes. When I turn on the kitchen light both voices yell, "Turn that off!"

Hope and Dr. Reeny sit cross-legged, hunched over a Ouija board.

"Hope has some news for you, Jack," Dr. Reeny says. "Sit down and place your hands over hers. We're trying to reach someone."

"Oh?" I say. "Has your therapy taken a new direction?"

Hope tugs the bottom of my leg and says, "Jack, this is serious."

I decide to play along and put my hand on Hope's. "By the way, Dealin' Dan gave us a minivan." Hope and Dr. Reeny lock eyes, slowly raising their hands to cover their mouths.

"Are you guys high?"

They laugh uncontrollably. Hope finally says, "No sweetie, I'm pregnant."

I fix my eyes on the board shimmering in the glow of the candles.

I'm not looking at her, but I can feel Hope trying to smile, about to cry.

"I thought you were on the pill."

Dr. Reeny puts her hand on my knee, "It happens."

Hope waits for a response.

"What should we do?" I say.

She grabs my hands and puts them on the Ouija board's wooden pointer. "Let's try this," she says.

Our attempts are imperfect at best. The board confirms Hope is pregnant, but answers "no" when asked if the baby will be a boy or a girl.

When Sarah leaves Hope hugs me and doesn't let go.

Disappearing acts are for magicians.

"Jack," she hugs me tighter. "I can't believe it's true."

I pull Hope into the kitchen, sit her down, and turn on all the lights. She looks confused and a little nervous as she watches me pace in front of her.

"Jack, what's going on? You're kinda scaring me."

"Well, in short, you just got pregnant behind my back, and I'm trying to figure out why."

"I can't believe you just said that. Take it back."

"I mean, I know your mother is *literally* trying to drive you crazy, but what I can't figure out is how getting pregnant will help." I lean against the counter, crossing my arms, staring at her.

She's biting her lower lip, blinking too often. I give her the meanest look I can muster, holding it for several seconds, then I start walking slowly in circles around the table. "You and your mother are like a living game of poker. You bluff each other, sometimes one of you folds, and every time you up the ante, she comes right back and raises you one."

I pause, because that was a great comparison.

"But what I want to know is, if this baby is your way of

raising the stakes, then what the hell is your mother gonna do back?"

Hope wipes at a tear that has run down the side of her face. "Because, Hope, it scares me to even think about it."

sorry

Mom's picking up our order at Sammy's. I'm sitting across the street, halfway down the block. Mom scoffed when she heard my reason for not going in.

"Where did I go wrong?" she said. "How did I raise a son who'd prefer to avoid a person, rather than apologize?" I shrugged; she continued, "He might not even be that upset with you. He's just a client."

"I know," I said. "I'm stupid. Just let me wait here."

With Hope waking up sick in the morning I'd been going by Sammy's earlier than usual. One morning Tim had written ALL IS FAIR IN WAR AND SANDWICHES. Another morning Sammy was there. He was in the back, but we made eye contact. He raised his hand as I started toward the entrance. I stopped. He pulled the door open a crack and said, "Not now, Jack. Stay away." He shook his head, turned the lock, and pulled down the shades. I had waited too long.

And he is not the only one: This morning Mom informed me Breach is engaged to her "beau." Sounds like she's pretty happy, so I guess I am too. There's an email from her waiting for me at home, but I can't bring myself to open it.

Mom crosses the street with our sandwiches in a bag. She's wearing khaki pants, a white baggy sweater, and sunglasses beneath a baseball hat. Halfway across, the traffic light changes and she jogs the final four strides to the sidewalk, looking almost ageless.

"I said hi to Sammy for you." She hands me the bag and goes through her purse for car keys. "I told him you moved to Texas to go to astronaut school." Smiling. "You're going to the moon."

"You didn't even talk to him."

"Did too. Would you rather I told him the truth?"

"Which is?"

"That you married rich, quit your job, and are too ashamed to tell him."

"Wow. That stings."

"Truth hurts."

We drive to a picnic area; lots of kids are running around making noise. Mom was quiet in the car, feeling guilty for being so mean, but refusing to say sorry because she knows she's right.

"So I was watching you cross the street," I say. "You looked like a kid."

She unwraps the paper around my sandwich and slides it across the table. "A kid?"

"It's a compliment, you looked good." I hand her a napkin. "You were pretty young when you had me, weren't you?"

"People had 'em young then. It's different now. You guys are smarter."

"So you regret having me so early?"

"I'll never regret giving birth to you. It was the happiest day of my life."

"So I wasn't an accident?"

"Accident? Where is this coming from?"

"You just said having children young is a bad idea, which is exactly what you did."

"Ever heard the phrase, hindsight is twenty-twenty?"

"You don't think I should have married Hope, do you?"

She looks at me, licks her lips, and sticks her sub as far into her mouth as possible.

"She's pregnant."

Mom's eyes bulge as she swallows more than she should. "How long?"

"A couple weeks."

"How'd it happen?"

"Seriously?"

"Well, did you plan it?"

"I didn't."

"Are you keeping it?"

"Probably."

"Her idea?"

"Most definitely."

"Did you even discuss it?"

"A little."

"What have you gotten yourself into?"

"I was hoping you'd tell me."

We finish lunch in almost-silence. I mash our wrappers and napkins into a ball, put them in the white paper bag and roll the top down. Neither of us stand because there's more talking to be done. Selfishly, I'd like to tell Mom about Dad, maybe get some sympathy, but she's heard enough for one day.

I haven't seen Dad since he broke up my fight with Tiny Tim. I'm pretty sure he left town. He sent me a letter that was postmarked from New Jersey. His note was short, but not sweet:

Jack,

My suspicions were confirmed: you've got a good little life going. A pretty, young wife, expensive house, and your older girlfriend isn't bad looking either. But really son, you should be more careful. That day at the pharmacy was a close call! I'd hate to see it all go down the drain . . . Details to follow . . . Stay tuned!

Love always,
Your dad.

Mom doesn't need to know this though, so I ask, "Do you want to go see the house?"

"Sure. But if it's as nice as you say, I think I'll be depressed."

"Because?"

"Because my twenty-seven-year-old son is living in a nicer house than mine."

"See. There are some advantages to marrying rich."

"I didn't mean what I said earlier."

"Yes you did, but it's fine. You're right. I should have never quit my job."

"You could get it back. You should have seen Sammy when he heard I was your mother, his eyes lit up."

"Did he say anything?"

"He said he's been waiting for you to see him. And he said to say sorry about the other morning, but he was in the middle of a meeting."

Hope is hunched over the kitchen table crying. She looks up, hair in a bun, the strap of a blue-and-white checkered apron hangs off her shoulder. The kitchen smells like smoke. All the lights are off and the windows open. A cookie sheet with charred gingerbread men smolders on the stove top. She says, "You're late," then in a nasty tone, "Snake-Eyes." She looks past me and sees my mother.

"Hope, are you all right?" Mom asks. "Oh, look at your cookies."

Hope's eyes slowly shift to the ruined gingerbread men. "I didn't set a timer because Mr. Snake-Eyed Jack said he'd be home by two. That's when they were supposed to come out."

A little confused why Hope keeps calling me Snake-Eyes, Mom is silent a moment before saying, "Jack's never on time. When I was pregnant I had to run up and down the stairs to break my water because he was three weeks overdue."

A heavy silence follows. Mom looks at the floor. I straighten a magnet on the refrigerator. Hope stares at us both.

"You told her."

"Hope—"

"—Did you tell her we don't have sex anymore too?"

"No."

"Did you tell her I was fat and eat like a pig?" She cries harder and looks at my mom. "Did you say, 'Mom, can a girl get pregnant even if she's on the pill?'"

Mom sits next to Hope, patting her shoulders and rubbing her back. Hope buries her head in her arms, her body convulsing as she struggles to breathe. She turns her head and glares at me from the corner of one eye.

Mom puts her arm across Hope's shoulders and leans toward her. "It's okay, everything's all right."

Hope lifts her head. "I know you didn't want Jack to marry me." Mom scowls at me. "Everyone said we had nothing in common. So many people were against us—it just made us want it more. We were stubborn, we were curious, and the second we were married I knew it was wrong."

Hope looks back down at the table. "I knew it would be hard, but I thought if we were strong enough, eventually, things would change."

"Hope," I say. "They still can. We'll figure it out."

"Know what Mom said when she saw the house?"

"You said she liked it."

"For ten minutes I followed her through every room. Then out to the porch, then to the garage. The whole time she didn't say a word. I followed her back inside, and as she poured two glasses of wine she said, 'Hopey, I'm proud of you. If only you could have married so well.'"

My mom gasps.

Hope continues, "That's when I decided to get pregnant." She blows her nose. "I figured if Jack was the father of her grandchild, she'd have to accept him."

I pull a chair next to Hope's. "Forget about your mom. You don't need her."

"Her husband died because of me. They were in love and she's never let me forget it. As if I could."

"You know that's not right, Hope. You don't owe her anything."

Hope gets up and washes her face in the kitchen sink. She wipes her forehead and cheeks with a dish towel. "My mother has resented me since I was nine years old. I don't want to treat my child the same way." She grabs a tray of the burnt cookies and dumps them in the garbage. "Who am I trying to kid?" she says, and heads toward the stairs.

A light rain falls as I walk Mom to her car. Mom rolls down her window and leans out the door before backing down our driveway. "Jack," she says, "keep an eye on her."

Back inside, the house is dark and the entire first floor still smells like burnt cookies. Our bedroom upstairs is empty; Hope has locked herself in the bathroom and won't come out, regardless of my pleas. She keeps telling me to leave her alone. Through the closed door her voice sounds almost as if she's in physical pain, but when I ask she says, "Just give me some space, please."

Feeling helpless I start to clean the kitchen but there isn't much to do. The cookie tray is blackened with hardened molasses so it stays in the garbage. I move on to the living room. I decide that now is as good a time as any to accept the news from Breach. I notice that the email has been opened, which is fine; Hope is sort of entitled since it is her email too, but obviously she knew the letter was for me. As I read Breach's words it becomes quite clear that today is not going to be a good day:

Jack,

You probably know by now that I'm engaged. How you take this news, I can only guess (Although I think deep down part of you will be a little upset) but I want to at least tell you how I feel.

I will always wonder "what if" when it comes to us, because I have loved you in a different and private way. The hard part is, I always will. I feel that we could have been happy together and who knows where that would have taken us. Now this is all irrelevant, but at least things are still good for us in that we've found other people who make us happy.

Maybe it was just timing . . . A creepy, sad, thought. I hope you will come to my wedding; you can sit next

to Alice and make sure she goes light on the wine at
the reception.

Love always,
Breach

Through the window I see the repairman for our broken
wall pull into the driveway. He's tall, freckled, and built in
a healthy way that suggests he was brought up on whole
milk, red meat, and values. He tells me to call him Charlie.

I show Charlie the room with the damaged wall and go
upstairs to check on Hope. She's finally come out of the
bathroom and is lying in bed.

When I ask if she's all right Hope shuts her eyes and
says, "Just leave me alone, okay Snake-Eyes?"

"That's the third time you've called me that. Want to tell
me why?"

"I think you're the one who needs to explain, Snake-
Eyes." She holds her hand up, showing four fingers.

Confused, I look into the bathroom and see a towel crumpled on the floor. Deciding to hang it, I enter the bathroom
and realize there's a lot more going on than I suspected: The
towel is covered in blood. In the sink is an empty bottle of
aspirin, its newly broken seal, and a ball of cotton, stuck to
the wet walls of the sink's basin.

I run to Hope, pull back the bed covers, and see a circle
of blood beneath her cloud-patterned pajamas. She barely
stirs and in a low, slow voice says, "Jack. Help me."

I carry her the way a groom carries his bride over the
threshold. On our way down the stairs Charlie emerges
from the damaged room saying, "I just need to go outside
to get some tools," before he processes the sight of Hope
crumpled in my arms, and shouts, "Good Lord!"

"Can you drive us to the hospital?"

Seconds later we're in the front seat of Charlie's pickup, speeding through the streets as he radios the ER on his CB that we're on our way and in serious need of help.

As we pull into the horseshoe-shaped emergency entrance two nurses are waiting with a gurney. They instruct me to leave Hope where she is and to step away. Right there in the truck they check for a pulse, shine a light in her both her eyes, and ask if she can hear them. She doesn't respond. One of the nurses, not the one who told me to step away, cuts the sides of Hope's pajama pants from the waist to the ankles and pulls them off. They do a quick check with the flashlight then lift her from the front seat onto the gurney, which has been pushed up against the truck. The whole process takes about ten seconds.

Hope is wheeled quickly inside and down a tan corridor. A woman tells me to follow her into an office. She's in her fifties, overweight, and wearing an aqua sweatshirt with *Florida* written in white script, neatly centered between two bending palm trees. She shows me a chair, hands me a clipboard with blank forms, and exits after telling me not to go anywhere.

A long time passes. After filling out the forms I get up and look down the hallway. No one looks familiar and I have no idea what's happened to Charlie. I tell myself Hope is all right, that Charlie and his CB were some kind of miracle. Unlike Mark's accident, we had time beat, and though my mind is filled with concern for Hope and the baby, I cannot help but make the distinction that Mark's death *was* accidental and what happened today was intentional.

• • •

Two hours have passed. Florida has peeked her head in twice to see that I haven't moved. The first time she took the forms, the second time she told me a doctor would be in shortly. A man wearing blue scrub pants and a collared shirt with a cross around his neck enters the room. He's tall, has black round glasses and a mustache.

"Your wife is no longer pregnant," he says. "She's alive and hemorrhaging slightly. Quite frankly she's very lucky. It looks as if she didn't do too much damage."

"Is she talking?"

"Yes. But she isn't telling the truth."

"What's she saying?"

The doctor leans against a cabinet with blue metal drawers. "According to her, she miscarried by natural causes and to dull the pain took some aspirin."

"Do you think she was trying to kill herself?"

"I don't know your wife but I can tell you that if someone spent five minutes searching the Internet they would learn that a heavy dose of aspirin can cause a miscarriage." He rubs his chin and plays with his mustache. "How long have you been married?"

"A little under a year."

"Was the pregnancy planned?"

"She'd been trying," I say.

"We're going to keep her overnight and have someone from our Psych department talk to her in the morning. Is there anyone you would like us to contact?"

"No. Can I see her now?"

Hope is pale and hooked to an IV. She waits until the doctor leaves the room to ask, "Did you call my mother? Please tell me you didn't."

I pull a chair up next to her bed and sit down. "Hope, what happened? I'm in shock."

"You're in shock? No Jack, shock is going to the supermarket to buy ingredients for gingerbread cookies and seeing a woman from your gym wearing your husband's favorite T-shirt. That's shock . . . Snake-Eyes."

"What are you talking about?"

"Jack, don't bother. I'm way too tired and honestly, I don't care. Really, it's a blessing in disguise. Now I can leave you without feeling guilty. But tell me, how long has it been going on?"

I could tell Hope the truth: that Merideth is just a friend and I stopped seeing her when Hope and I got married, but with my best poker face I bluff, "I started seeing Merideth at about the same time I figured out you were having an affair with James Kidder."

"Are you losing your mind?"

"Actually, for a while I thought I was. But really, Hope, having an affair with a man you met on our honeymoon?"

"Jack, I don't even know James Kidder. I met him once, briefly, on the beach. Don't try to turn the tables." She shakes her head disapprovingly.

"You've only met James Kidder once?"

"You were with me, remember?"

"So who was the guy in Aspen? A James Kidder impersonator?" Hope looks stunned. She has no idea how I know about her and Kidder meeting in Aspen. Her speechlessness confirms her guilt and for the first time it truly dawns on me that Tianna wasn't lying.

Hope doesn't like my tone. She looks as if she's on the edge of cracking and I think it's because this conversation is really about the end of our marriage.

"Believe what you want, Jack, but I'm telling you there's nothing going on between me and James Kidder."

"He called our house. I answered the phone. He left his phone number. You don't think I'd recognize his voice?"

Hope looks like she's about to cry, but I don't feel sorry for her. All I want to do is make her cry.

"So tell me, how much money did we get when you married me?"

"Who told you about the money?"

"Tianna let it slip at Bunny's New Year's Eve party. And swallowing a bunch of aspirin? That's a really fucked up perception of birth control."

Hope is sucking on the bottom corner of her lip.

"And don't blame that one on your crazy mom."

I can't stop myself from grabbing her hand. "Remember our first date, when we saw those two kids and we ended up talking about what's Real versus what's Ideal?"

She nods.

"Well just once I'd like to see them happen at the same time."

Hope raises an eyebrow. "I read the email from Breach. Maybe that's where you should be looking."

"Do you really want to give up that easily?"

"Jack, we've known for a long time this could never work."

The doctor knocks on the door lightly. He tells me to leave in a minute. Hope agrees and says nothing else because there is nothing else to say.

Leaving the hospital I see Charlie in the waiting room, reading a *Life* magazine. He looks up when I call his name, then quickly stands.

"Is everything all right?" He asks.

"Charlie, have you been waiting here the whole time?"

He looks slightly embarrassed and says, "What hap-pened?"

I tell him I'll explain everything on the ride home—it's a long story—but basically, Hope is going to be just fine.

scrabble

Hope left the day after she returned from the hospital. She was gone before I woke up, but kind enough to write a note. *Jack, I'm leaving for ten days. Be gone when I get back.*

She'll be home tomorrow.

Dad has been calling constantly, but thanks to Caller ID I can not only skip his calls, but also be sure he's still in New Jersey. I copied down his number on a piece of paper and stuck it in my wallet because soon it will come in handy; for now though he can wait.

Hope's mother wouldn't say where she had gone. I called Kidder's number. The voicemail said, "I'll be out of town for three months. Call my cell if you've got that number." No name, just the famous voice.

Mom said come home ten days ago. She called every morning Hope was gone. "At least get out of the house," she said after a week. "Go for a walk. Do something." On the ninth night she came over unannounced with a bag of sandwiches and a six-pack of beer.

I followed her to the kitchen. "How was work?"

"I should be asking you that. I know you're sad, Jack, but I gotta be honest. I thought you were much stronger than this."

"Why are you saying this?"

"Jack, I love you, but it's time to come back from la-la land. Now come on."

"La-la land? Mom, there's been a lot of crap going on in my life that you don't even know the half of. So don't tell me about la-la land. At least I tried. La-la land is sitting around with the same five women every Friday night complaining about how lonely you are, but never doing anything to fix it."

"Turn this on me if it'll make you feel better, but everyone told you from the start that you and Hope had no chance." Mom rolls her eyes. "Regardless of her money."

"Seeing Mark die, the way he did, alive one minute and gone the next—life is *totally* uncertain. And if that's the case, why be certain about anything you do?"

"Jack you have to understand something right now. People die. It's a fact, not an excuse. Write it on your hand if you have to, but remember it because enough is enough already."

She left. There were three sandwiches in the bag and the note "Don't forget to eat. —Love, Mom."

After eating, a walk seemed like a good idea. The streets were empty. Signs for politicians were stuck in yards; dogs stared out from porches. Hope offered the Ideal. She was pretty, fun, financially independent and she had a clear vision of the kind of life she wanted to lead. We were young so maybe it was a gamble, but what isn't? People do change, and it can happen overnight, and then suddenly, after three months or twenty years, the marriage is over, or it begins anew.

I kept walking. Never in my life had I been thought of as being from "the wrong side of the tracks." Hope comes from a world few people know of, a world inherently incestuous because no one is good enough except for those already included. When I met Hope I didn't know this, but as time passed I ignored the warning signs.

A traffic light stopped me. It was time to turn around.

At home I stood at the foot of our driveway. Inside, only the kitchen lights were on. Hope was returning the next day. I tried to say good-bye to the house, like when a little kid looks through the back window of his station wagon the day his family moves to a new town. "Good-bye house," I said and it was so hollow, so insincere, that I shivered, embarrassed, angry that I could allow myself to be such an idiotic loser.

Hope comes through the front door holding a suitcase in each hand. She sees me watching television, eating pizza from a box on the coffee table.

She drops both bags at the same time and says, "Why are you still here?"

Still looking at the television, "Where've you been?"

"Actually Jack, I'm glad you're here. I'd like to smooth things out so we can end this on a civil note."

"You look tan."

"I was in the sun."

"Are you going to tell me who you were with, or do I have to read about it in *People* magazine?"

Hope squats over her suitcase, zipping it open. Her skirt slides all the way up her newly tanned thighs and she does nothing to cover herself. "My mother's going to be here tomorrow. She wants to meet with you."

"And you want to end on a civil note?"

"Things just got way out of control." Hope digs through her suitcase, pulling out clothes, a pink bikini, and one of her sheer nightgowns. "I'd like it if we could part without you feeling too bitter."

"Sweety," I say, "I'm gonna be just fine. Pardon my French, but you're the one that's fucked."

Hope stares at me, smirking. Then she chuckles with the severe condescension only possessed by pretty, rich girls. "Care to explain?"

"Sure you can handle it?"

She tries another chuckle but it's less effective.

"Hope: You . . . will never . . . be happy. You own everything in the world and it's not enough. You think getting married and buying a house will close the door on a bad childhood. You and your mother are a pair of rare birds, honey, and if you don't work things out, one of you is gonna go extinct."

Hope is laughing. She walks over, puts her arms around me, and kisses my mouth. Her tongue licks my shut lips. I turn my head, wiping my mouth off with my hand.

She pushes off my shoulder and says, "Good night, Jack. You can pick my mother up at noon."

I call Merideth from a pay phone at a twenty-four-hour gas station. A white guy with blond dreadlocks and leather sandals sits on the pavement, trading bites of a burrito with his Labrador retriever. He catches me staring so I wave and he looks away.

Merideth sits on the curb in front of her house. Her hug is accented with alcohol breath. She walks unsteadily, trying to look sober. Two plastic pink flamingos are stuck into the ground along a wooden plank leading to her front door.

"My friends did that in the middle of the night before my birthday. They drove my husband crazy so I left them there." She throws the door open too hard and it bounces back into her.

Through the front hallway, we pass a kitchen with red brick tiles and move out onto a wooden patio above a small stream. The evening air is cool. Merideth sits on a metal chair, waiting for me to speak.

"So how've you been?" I say.

"I've been better."

"Where is everyone?"

"Everyone's gone."

"Gone where?"

"I told my husband to leave. The kids are with their grandmother."

"He moved out? For good?"

"Almost."

"What do you think?"

She lets out a deep breath and closes her eyes. "I think . . . I think I waited way too long."

"And now?"

"I start over. Back to square one. Sorry about Hope."

"Looks like we're in the same boat."

"Different bodies of water though."

"I'm not sure I understand."

"I'll tell you tomorrow."

She leaves me on the porch. After a while I go back into the house.

Her underwear, peach silk, hangs off the stairwell banister. At the top of the stairs shirt sleeves point left. Outside a cracked door a dress lies crumpled. One flickering candle shows her beneath a puffy blanket pulled up to her neck.

"Oop!" She says. "Found me."

I lie down, all my clothes still on, and roll her to hold her from the back. She curls into me. My arm reaches underneath her, wrapping around her stomach. The other strokes her hair.

"What did you mean on the porch?"

She's tired and drunk and on the verge of passing out. "Jack, honey. We're at different places in our lives. You said yourself it could never work. Just hold me for a while, but you gotta leave soon."

"Merideth?"

"Shh."

Her breathing slows. She wiggles and her foot twitches. Within minutes she's snoring lightly. I kiss her ear, say thank you, and shut my eyes, enjoying the soft rhythm of her breath.

"Get up!" She yells, pushing my shoulder hard.

Still half asleep, "What?"

"My husband. He just drove up."

They say people can lift cars if trapped underneath. About halfway down the stairs I leap, bending my knees upon contact with the floor, making no sound while at the same time snatching Merideth's peach underwear off the banister, disposing of evidence, already making new strides toward the back door. Over the porch I land in the creek, and splash through it until I reach a park fifty yards downstream.

The park is a small rectangle of grass with a swing set in the corner. Not far away a middle-aged man wearing an army shirt and blue jeans sits on a bench. My watch says quarter-of-six, A.M. The Continental is still parked in front of Merideth's but will have to stay there until her husband leaves. The man on the bench is hunched over several small Tupperware containers. Three brown paper bags rest at his feet, from which he pulls and replaces more plastic cases.

"Mind if I sit here?" I ask him. My feet and legs are soaked.

He looks up, his mouth slightly open. He slides to one

side and hands me a round container. I can feel marbles rolling around inside the bin. "What you been up to boy?"

Since I don't feel like telling him about almost getting busted lying in bed with a married woman by her husband, I ask, "What are you doing with the marbles?"

"Organization. Military taught me that. There's not a lot we can control in this world, but we can be organized. What's your excuse?"

In less than a minute this homeless man has been able to determine the unbalanced status of my life. I repeat his question in my head: "What's your excuse?" And for a moment I see myself sitting there on the bench, and realize I have no excuse.

I ask him, "What are you doing today?"

"Serving soup."

"By the old movie theater, right?"

When the Veteran's Shelter was built the owner of the theater did everything in her power to prevent its construction. She was a good client, always bought at least a third of a page, sometimes more if the new movies were blockbusters. She was afraid the shelter's inhabitants would deter people from wanting to stand in line to buy tickets. Everyone criticized her, but six months after the building was finished she had to move because people stopped coming. The theater's still vacant.

The next hour is spent on a different bench just a few blocks away. I take off my socks and shoes so they'll dry quicker. Then it's back to square one.

"It's about time. Sammy's out back. Want me to get him?" Jimmy's holding a foot-long roll in one hand, a knife in the other.

"That's all right, Jimmy, I'll go back there myself."

The last two inches of a cigar is wedged between Sammy's thumb and forefinger. Two men in shiny, double-breasted suits are unloading packaged meat from a white, unmarked refrigerated truck. Sammy sees my shadow and turns around quickly.

"Do I know you?" He says, pointing his cigar. "Because you look familiar, but the guy I know is smart enough not to come back here after being gone so long."

"I'm sorry, Sammy. I don't know what to say."

"Well you better say something."

As Sammy listens all his comments are in the form of questions. "Dr. Reeny? What kind of a name is that? . . . Fruit beer? You gotta be kidding me . . . Dealin' Dan? You mean the guy who dresses up as an alien?" And finally, "Aspirin, huh?"

"It was the second worst thing I've ever seen."

Sammy thinks a minute, probably about his own past. My trials *ain't nothin'*.

"So what do you want from me, Jack? What am I supposed to do here?"

"Well, are you still putting ads in the paper?"

"Yeah, of course. No offense, Jack, but life goes on."

"How's the new guy?"

"The new guy? He's alright. He don't clean my windows out of the goodness of his heart or nothin', but he gets the job done and doesn't disappear for months on end."

"I understand." I shake his hand and take a few steps backward. "And Sammy, I'm really sorry about everything. You mean a lot more to me than I've been able to show you."

He lets me take a few steps before calling out, "You know, Jack, that new guy kinda spits a lot when he talks.

It's very unsanitary; spit flying all over the deli every time he opens his mouth. I should probably talk to his boss, what with flu season approaching."

"Sammy, I swear, I'll never mess up again."

"You messed up enough the first time." He looks at his loafers, bends down and smudges a spot in the leather. "You're a good kid though. Why don't you come by Tuesday? We'll see what we can do."

"I don't know what to say, Sammy."

"You already said that. And Jack, thanks for keeping an eye on the place while I was gone. The guys next door complained about you taking all their napkins."

"Should I go apologize?"

"No. I took care of it."

Hope's mother is waiting outside and walks to the curb before the car even stops. She gets in the front seat and says, "This shouldn't take long."

I'm late. Walking from Merideth's to Sammy's and back wasn't part of my original agenda. My hair is tangled, yesterday's clothes smell like creek water. Hope's mother cracks the window and tells me the address of a lawyer's office.

"So what do you think about your daughter dating a movie star? Pretty exciting."

"She told you?"

"Are you gonna hit on him too? Maybe you guys can like, do a remake of *Mrs. Robinson* or something."

"From what I hear, Jack, *you're* the one who likes older women."

"But you wouldn't know yourself, now would you?"

"And for that, I am quite thankful." She looks at me from the corners of her eyes and smiles.

"You're quite something, that's for sure, but getting back to the present, I don't want any money if that's what this is all about."

"That's very nice of you, Jack, but legally we need to cover some things. You people can be very finicky when it comes to such matters."

"*You people?* So what did Hope say about the baby?"

"She miscarried. It happens all the time."

"Timely, wouldn't you say?"

"You guys were a mismatch from the beginning. At least one thing worked out."

"That's quite a silver lining."

"Considering the cloud, I would say so." She folds her hands and smiles.

"How do you do it? Are you blind and deaf or do you have some incredible ability to walk through life unconscious?"

"Hope is all I have left. I have to look out for her."

"Well you should leave her alone because you're ruining her life."

"You don't need to worry about Hope anymore; it's not your place."

"I'll always care about her. Regardless of my place."

"As you will. But from a distance, I'd imagine."

"Did someone switch your Valium with bitch pills?"

"Jack, you're so clever. All this time I've underestimated you. Turn the car around, quick! We've got a marriage to fix!"

She's laughing now, but she won't be for long. Armed with the incorrectly dated prenuptial agreement, an argument will be made that I'm entitled to half the money Hope inherited when we were married. I smile, wink, and turn the radio to a lively Top 40 station.

•   •   •

The lawyers are a father-and-son duo, both six feet tall, in good shape, and handsome. The son is no older than thirty. Their secretary is balding. He's new on the job. He doesn't greet us, and when the son notices through his office door, he scolds the man and says, "You *do* know how to make coffee, don't you?" Entering the meeting room we catch his father watching golf on a small television.

Hope's mother hasn't spoken since the car. The four of us sit at one corner of a long black table on black leather chairs that spin. They offer thirty-five thousand dollars, a little more than my salary for a year of work at the paper. I play the scene like I'm not interested in taking any money. My instincts tell me that Hope's mother will leave this "petty situation of financial matters" once she thinks all is safe. A town car was parked outside the office when we pulled up, waiting to take her home. The only reason she rode here with me was for one last chance to let me know that I don't belong near her daughter.

"More than generous," Hope's mother says, signing first, then standing. "Jack, I'm happy there will be no problems here. Everyone has suffered enough already. Good-bye."

After double-checking her signatures the father hands the contracts to his son and says, "You can handle this from here." Then to me, "Thanks for your cooperation."

The son taps the bottoms of the pages against the table so they fall into a neat stack. He rolls his chair backwards, spins one-and-a-half times, and curls the papers into a tight cylinder and holds it to one eye, like a telescope. On the window sill behind him is a picture of him and his father standing on a boat, floating on a clear ocean. Hanging from the son's hand is a four-foot-long sailfish on a hook.

"Like I said. I don't want their money. You may not

understand." I'm stalling to give Hope's mother enough time to get in the town car and be driven away.

"I understand. They got a word for you in law school . . . Chump."

"Did you catch that big fish all by yourself?"

He spins around and slaps the papers down. "It took over three hours to reel that sucker in. He put up a hell of a better fight than you."

"Yeah but you're their lawyer, so what do you care?"

"Just sign the papers and get out of here."

I smile like we're both in on a private joke. "You like a good battle, don't you?"

"I'm a lawyer aren't I?"

"Well you got one. He likes to be called the Gooseman. I'll have him call you tomorrow." Not signing the papers, I stick his pen in the front pocket of my shirt, turn toward the door, calling over my shoulder, "You better strap yourself in for this one."

When I call Dad's number from the Caller ID I get a hotel. Fortunately Dad is still booked and when the receptionist puts me through he answers.

"Dad, it's Jack. Be honest with me for a second. Do you know a midget named Tiny Tim?"

"Wait a minute, I think I know this joke."

"It's not a joke. Have you been conspiring with him?"

"*Conspiring,* with a midget named Tiny Tim? Jack, have you gone completely mad?"

"Actually, I was wondering the same about you. You call yourself the Gooseman even though no one else does; you dress up like Five-O and park outside my house the hottest week of the year; you've got some sidekick flunky named Gill who threatened me about my wife; and you send me bizarre letters that either ask for forgiveness or threaten to blackmail me. Explain yourself, please."

"Well Jack, it's quite simple. You made a phone call from the hotel room during your recent visit. It was a long distance phone call that lasted well over an hour. Suffice it to say I wasn't pleased when I got the bill. However, I kept the phone number for my personal records."

My voice is raised to a shout, "Did you call Merideth? Because she got beat up and if you caused that, I swear to God, Dad, I'll come after you myself!"

Calmly he replies, "Don't get ahead of yourself, boy. Of course I didn't call her, that would ruin what we call leverage. I may have tracked her down and followed her around, but let's get back to your phone call. It cost me fifty dollars, but if you pay me back, plus a little something I call 'Secrecy Tax,' I'll be willing to forget about the whole thing."

Only because I'm curious I ask, "How much?"

"Ten grand."

"Well I got bad news for you, Dad. Hope and I are getting divorced, so it kinda looks like your 'Secrecy Tax' just went way down in value."

Smoothly, and not missing a beat he answers, "You see, that's where my leverage comes in, son. I'm sure you'd like to keep your phone call a secret from Merideth's husband as well."

"Too late for that too, Dad. You know you really should get out of gambling. Your timing sucks."

A long silence follows and when Dad finally speaks his voice is much lower, and slowed way down. "Well could you at least send me the fifty dollars? I need it."

"I tell you what, Dad. I'm getting thirty-five thousand as

goodbye money from the divorce. I signed a prenup but check the dates—it isn't valid. Drag it out as long as you can and I promise they'll pay up just to get you out of their hair. Start with the mother, she's where the real money's at."

"And what do you want from me?"

"Leave me and Mom alone. For good. No phone calls, no letters, no nothing. Just stay away."

"Jack. It pains me to hear you talk like that."

"Do you want the money or not?"

"Send me the prenup and give me the lawyer's number."

"So this is it, Dad. Forever."

He hangs up before I say goodbye.

Hope wants my stuff out of the house by five, three hours from now. The Continental still smells like the perfume Hope and her mother both wear. On the dashboard is a baby blue hair scrunchy. The floor of the back seat is littered with empty diet soda cans and fashion magazines. I throw them out; the scrunchy too. But clinging to the seats' upholstery are strands of Hope's hair, and even with all the doors open the scent of perfume lingers. I try driving with the windows down. Nothing works.

On the side of the road I call Breach from a pay phone without the slightest idea of what to say if she picks up.

"Bonjour," is how she answers the phone, her voice excited with cheer.

"Breach?" The traffic makes it difficult to hear.

"Jack? Did you hear, is that why you're calling?"

"Of course I heard; you sent me an email." And this I decide will be my reason for calling her: to thank her for her nice letter and tell her I feel the same way. To tell her all the mistakes I've made and how sorry I am, for both of us. I'll explain that I'm happy for her and unjustifiably sad for myself. And then, pretending to joke I'll say that if anything happens I'll be here waiting. "Just give me the word and I'll come and get you at the altar," I'll say, chuckling.

"Not that," she's almost yelling. "Paris. We're moving to Paris." I'm silent so she continues to explain that her "beau" has been transferred. I'm still silent; she can probably hear the cars in the background. "Jack? Can you hear me?"

"Yeah. Hey, that's great. I've never even been to Paris."

"You sound funny. Where are you?"

"I'm on the side of the road killing time." The operator asks for more change, of which I have none, so we're disconnected.

Outside the veteran's shelter a group of hunched men smoke, their eyelids heavy and drooping. Inside, the man from the park is serving soup, his paper bags placed safely beside the metal legs of a brown foldout table. He doesn't recognize me even though I'm wearing the same clothes.

The director's office is on the second floor. His door is open as he talks on the phone, seated at his desk. His head is completely bald, a scar two inches long makes a purple line above an ear; a gray turtleneck matches the color of his handlebar mustache. After his conversation he waves his hand and greets me by rolling from his desk in a wheelchair.

"Do you take donations?"

"What have you got in mind?"

"I got a Lincoln Continental fully loaded in good condition with low miles."

"Why?"

I hand him the keys. "The car's parked right out front.

There's nothing wrong with it. The driver needs all the work."

I knock on the door to be official. Hope answers wearing a white scarf around her head, tied in a knot beneath her chin, with a black pair of sunglasses perched on top. Just beyond the door my bags are already packed in the hallway. She's wearing nonprescription glasses, her finger stuck in the pages of a magazine, saving her place.

"Well don't you look Hollywood," I say.

"I packed your stuff."

"Mind if I take a look around?"

Hope puts her magazine down. "Honestly, Jack. I think I got it all."

"You forgot one thing." She follows me up the stairs. "My Buddha."

"Honey," she says.

"Do you mind if I have a second? I swear I won't take anything. You can search me if you want."

She smiles. "I'll be downstairs."

Hope's room is a mess. Empty picture frames scatter the floor, the old photos of us stacked in a shoebox. Unpacked clothes droop from open suitcases in a corner. Standing in the doorway I listen for a sound from downstairs. A cork squeaks, pulled from a bottle in the kitchen.

Hope's underwear drawer is divided into three rows; colors on one side, white on the other, and black in the middle. Merideth's peach underwear is wrinkled from being in my pocket all day, but smoothes out nicely as I spread them across the precisely folded stacks Hope had arranged with so much care.

Downstairs I ask if I can call a cab.

"Where's your car?"

"Sold it. I need the money."

Hope sits down at the breakfast table. "You know what? Why don't you keep the minivan? Really, you can have it."

Flipping through the Yellow Pages for a car service I say, "I'll be all right."

"Seriously. I want you to have it. I wasn't planning on keeping it anyway. I mean, it *is* a *minivan*."

I shut the book. "Yeah?"

Suddenly very happy with herself she stands up quickly, handing me the keys from the counter. "This is good," she says.

The interior still smells like new car. The far backseat folds nicely and pushes forward on wheels, making maximum storage space with ease. My two duffle bags are thrown on the backseat, the Buddha sits shotgun. The garage door is still down. I wave to Hope from the driver's side window. She waves back, pushing the button so the door will go up.

My hand on the steering wheel still wears a ring. I call Hope over to the window.

"What?" She says.

Putting my ring in her hand I say, "Watch this for me while I'm gone."

Hope smirks.

"And one other thing, tell your mother to give my best to the Gooseman."

At the bottom of the driveway the gears switch from reverse to drive, jerking the Buddha until the transmission settles and as a unit we roll forward.

life

The stool waggles, one leg shorter than the other two. White vinyl sails neutralize the spotlights, but my shadow flutters behind the camera, covering most of the wall across from me.

"This isn't in my job description," I say.

Deb and Trixy are my newest clients. Peppy blonde women from Texas: both in their late twenties, wearing designer clothes that match the color of their eye shadow. They run a dating service, Love Sleuth. The company is quite successful. This is the seventh city they've launched. According to the brochure, the first six have been huge successes, matching several happy new couples. As for Deb and Trixy, both remain single.

They're working out the kinks in the video system, using me as a guinea pig. Love Sleuth is buying the biggest advertising package our newspaper offers, a ten-week commitment, the first ad a full page, then dwindling in size as the weeks progress. Landing them got me back in the good graces of my boss, who upon my return said, "Well, if it isn't the Son of Sammy."

Sammy was the only old client I got to keep; my boss has

given me six weeks to find new business. If I don't bring in a certain amount, I'm out.

Trixy says, "We haven't signed the final contract, so officially this isn't your job."

"Are you trying to blackmail me? Because it's been done before."

A banner hangs across the backdrop. The slogan *"Tired of playing games? Let Love Sleuth do your footwork"* is punctuated on either side by a heart with arms, holding a magnifying glass.

Deb hands me a fill-in-the-blank script, a cue card for a would-be customer. "You can read from this."

"My name is Jack. I'm twenty-seven years old and sell advertising space for a newspaper. It's a decent job. I'm looking for a woman who can ride a unicycle while juggling bowling pins. My hobbies are giving myself vertigo and gymnastics. Biggest turn-on: a well-balanced meal. Libra."

Trixy turns off the camera, "Wow, Jack, what emotional depth."

"Honestly, I'm just like everyone else. I want the person I care about to care about me. Anything extra is a bonus."

Love Sleuth's office is still unfurnished, the space was previously occupied by a tanning salon. Deb reads the instructions off the handle of a carpet cleaner she rented from a supermarket. She's hoping a steam clean will get rid of the lingering smell of suntan lotion.

There's something sexy about her handling of the carpet cleaner. Maybe it's the blazer and short skirt.

"The smell's pretty strong," I say. "You might have to repaint."

"Forget that. I'll just pretend I'm at the beach."

I shut my eyes and sniff. "That could work. Play some calypso music and you're set."

• • •

My next stop is the newsstand for a fresh pack of mints. The day's papers are stacked at the foot of the counter. The tabloids are stuffed in a rack at eye level. Nausea hits. "Lewd Kidder Rebounds With Nude Babe On Beach" is the head-line above a black-and-white picture of a UFO that looks more like a drawing than a photograph.

I take a seat on a restaurant stoop. Just a few pages deep Hope is there in the raw, lying on a towel, propped on her elbows, sunning her back. Another photo is a frontal; Hope wading in the tropical water. They're almost tasteful, minus the black censor bars and the fact that they'd been taken with a telephoto lens from behind a bush by an entrepreneurial dirt-bag who no doubt just made a bundle.

A man's voice. "Excuse me, may I ask if you're voting in next week's election?"

Without looking up from the paper. "Haven't really thought about it yet."

"Not enough young people exercise their right. You have a voice, use it."

A button on his blazer says BINDER in big red letters. In smaller blue ink is the name Joe. Joe Binder is a former weatherman from a local television station.

I look up at the sky. "You think it's gonna rain this week-end?"

He frowns. "I see a troubled young man, sitting on the pavement, reading the tabloids."

"Are you psychic? 'Cause you could probably write for this paper."

"I can't predict the future—"

"—At least not the weather—"

"—But I believe I can change it. Proper planning prevents

poor performance. Listen to me good, son. If you believe what you do today won't affect what happens tomorrow, you'll be sitting on this stoop for the rest of your life. I'm sure you didn't get here by accident. Even if it's not for me, do yourself a favor and vote this Tuesday."

Binder crosses the street handing out fliers, Hope and James Kidder romp through the surf, and a brown spotted cat debates whether or not to approach and rub up against my legs.

It's Friday morning. I came to show Sammy his ad for the weekend and make sure he's happy. In honor of his home-land, and because of another distribution screwup, he's offering a buy one–get one free on twelve-inch Italian subs. He's run this special before; it's always very popular and it kills the competition.

I ask Sammy if he wants to know who wrote the messages on his windows. He says he doesn't care. Sitting behind his desk, dressed in a sharp suit, a cigar hanging from the corner of a clenched mouth, he counts stacks of cash from different manila envelopes and explains: "People think I used to be in the Mafia, Jack. I don't like it, but the rumors are better for business than any ad in a newspaper. No offense."

Sammy raises his eyebrows, sliding mints across his desk. I let the tin sail completely over the edge before I catch it.

"You want to go next door and get some coffee?"

Sammy tilts his head and scrunches his eyes inquisitively, "What's a matter? You don't like Jimmy's coffee?"

"No. It's good. I just thought you might want to get out of here for a while."

"You don't gotta lie to me, Jack. Jimmy's coffee is terri-ble. Just don't tell him I said so."

"Your secret's safe with me, Sammy."

"I know, Jack." He pats my back. "I know."

"Thank God it's Friday!" Alice sits on my mother's couch, holding out her glass of wine. The Drinking Club lives on, all the members intact, their problems with men a perpetual revolving door of same old stories. They survive by sending each other funny cards through the mail that say things like, "Who needs sex when you've got a great pair of shoes?" All the women know about Hope. They're relieved to see it's over but they're sensitive enough not to mention it. Yet.

I finally told Mom about Dad. Her reaction to my giving him the prenuptial papers was simple. "You're an idiot," she said. "Not only is that like giving an alcoholic the keys to a liquor store, but it doesn't accomplish anything. His word means nothing."

I responded, "Mine does, and now he knows how I feel. It's worth it."

For the most part, though, living with Mom has been good. We wake up and leave for work at the same time. The forty-minute commute is a drag, but the minivan helps. It handles better than the Continental and has a CD player.

The Drinking Club does not acknowledge Hope's debut in the tabloids today, but I get a phone call from Tianna, who has seen the pictures. She alludes to our night in New York City, saying it's too bad since I'm no longer married. Music plays behind her. She says she's in her kitchen, mixing frozen drinks with her friends. I almost thank her for tipping me off about the inheritance and for clueing me in about James Kidder, but I really don't feel that grateful. Tianna tells me to call her next time I'm in New York, but I tell her I'm not interested in trying to get back at my ex-wife by sleeping with her best dysfunctional friend. Tianna laughs, says I'm "priceless," and blows a kiss into the phone before hanging up.

Breach shows up. Alice must have invited her. When I open the door Breach says without pausing a beat, "James Kidder, huh?"

"Did you ever think he and I would end up in the same sentence?"

Breach shrugs. "He's got bad skin."

"That's what I hear. Are you coming inside?"

"No. I just wanted to show my face. I'll be here next week though. You?"

"I think so. When are you off to Rome?"

"Paris, stupid. Like you didn't know." She laughs, shaking her head, trying to frown at me. "I'm not going."

She doesn't offer an explanation and I don't ask for one.

There is something perversely seductive about the way she stands. Her arms are crossed, her head tilted sideways, like she's daring me to do something she may or may not consent to.

"Sure you don't want to come in?" I say.

"Next week."

"Alright. Next week it is."

Before she turns to leave she steps inside and hugs me quickly, saying, "It's good to have you back . . . Jack." Then she laughs at how stupid it sounds and jogs away.

We were lost. Forty-five seconds before the wreck we made a U-turn in one of the empty dirt road's intersections. Mark was in the lead. He turned first and for a moment we both stopped, our cars facing opposite directions, the driver's side windows just a few feet apart. He smiled, shrugging his shoulders, enjoying the uncertainty of our course, then sped in the direction from which we had already come.

breach's rules

The guys in New York tell me to move, but leaving town is not the answer. Their arguments are persuasive—change of scenery, new faces, better career. I miss my friends, but a new environment would do nothing for my problems. I have to find the place that rattles in dead-silent darkness until it has fed too long on nervous thought; where strength is born, hard decisions made, voice is discovered; the very place where all the pain shall be healed.

Breach is reminding me that all this could have been avoided. It's Friday night and we're at my mother's. The Drinking Club got a little crazy and all the women went out on the town. Alice convinced everyone to go swing dancing at a nightclub called The Church. Breach and I cleaned up and now we're sitting on the kitchen counters.

"Think about it, Jack. The two relationships you chose, Hope and *Merideth*," Breach rolls her eyes as she says Merideth's name. "Both had no future. And you knew it."

"Don't roll your eyes at Merideth."

"Puh-lease, she's ten years older than you, Jack."

"Life is one mistake after another, Breach. You might as well enjoy it."

Breach gets up and starts to fill two glasses with water.

"Look, in a way, I understand your reaction to Mark's death." She hands me a glass. "But still, there's a fine line between living life like it's tenuous and acting like a twerp."

"So now I'm a twerp?"

"No. Now you're nothing."

"Nothing?"

"You got a clean slate, Jack."

Breach hops back up on the counter. I walk over and stand in front of her. "What's your slate look like?"

"Spotless."

"Let's go for a walk. It's nice out."

The D.C.'s cars are parked in a nice row along the curb. They all climbed in the minivan to go to The Church. Breach is still inside turning off the lights. She asks if we should lock the door. I don't answer.

"Jack," she says. "Are you there?"

"More than ever, baby. More than ever."

Breach shuts the door and grabs my hand. It's nice out. We could probably walk all night.

acknowledgments

I would like to thank the following:

My agent, Meredith Phelan (Linda Chester & Associates): Sold this book, a feat several agents before her deemed improbable, which can only mean that she's got more game than all of them.

My editor, Brant Rumble: Changed the title, cut twenty percent of the manuscript and wrote the book's funniest joke about whether or not it is possible to *sound* horny. In short, Brant is The Man, and if they'd let me, I'd call him my coauthor.

My teachers: Mary Caponegro, Keith Abbott, Bobby Louise Hawkins, Randi Davenport, Kirsten Wasson, Kristen Iverson.

Patty Stout: For her support, love, and ideas.

Lisa Olsen: For her morning doses of inspiration.

The consulting firm Woods, Goodman, Tiedemann, Connell & Leness: For advice that was sometimes good, sometimes bad, and sometimes unsolicited (hey bud).

Copyeditors, M. C. Hald and Charles Naylor: They must wonder how I ever graduated high school.

Scott Focker Phillips: For giving me a job that allowed

me to work on this book, and for never failing to crack me up.

My entire family, who, above all, matter most.

I'd also like to thank: Katherine "Shuggie" Robertson; Thomas May; Phillip Barnhart; Naropa University MFA Prose Track; Patsy Tarr and *2wice* magazine; Robert L. Chapman (editor of my thesaurus); Megan Rapaglia MA, RN, CS, ANP; Marie Gentile; Paul Kieth; F. Jackie; Rally Sport; Fourteenth Street Bar and Grill; Boulder Open Space; and, without a doubt, Ron Kleinsmith at Casa Alvarez.